SPACESHIP UNDERGROUND

SPACESHIP UNDERGROUND

Science and Technology Are Limited
to the Elements That Exist Now

METİN ŞAHİN

Library of Congress Control Number: 2024916699
ISBN: Hardcover   978-1-6698-9109-3
                 Softcover   978-1-6698-9108-6
                 eBook   978-1-6698-9107-9

Print information available on the last page.

Rev. date: 08/14/2024

To order additional copies of this book, contact:
Xlibris
UK TFN: 0800 0148620 (Toll Free inside the UK)
UK Local: (02) 0369 56328 (+44 20 3695 6328 from outside the UK)
www.Xlibrispublishing.co.uk
Orders@Xlibrispublishing.co.uk
862136

In this study, I will try to examine the universe and its perception by living beings (especially humans) from the universe to living beings and from living beings to the universe. In this sense, we can isolate a human being from the universe in which he or she exists and evaluate it from a different perspective. With this approach, very different results emerge. In the same way, we can think that this situation is transferred to everything that is a human product. Just like some traits are passed on from parents to their children. The approach is as follows: In reality, apart from the living beings we know (humans, animals, plants, etc.), nothing else is physically tangible, that is, it is abstract. Humans perceive this intangible with their sense organs and give it meaning/ meanings after the formations that occur in their brains, so that the universe that they know as concrete exists only in their own minds. (Note: As mentioned above, this is a different way of evaluation contrary to what is known). As such, conflicts that occur between people can be said to be "because of this". Whatever pushes the limits of human thought is treated as plus infinity and minus infinity. However, this is not because they are infinite, but because human thought has a limited capacity. In fact, the object (?) touched by a human being is not actually in its known form, but the spontaneous formation of that known form in line with the characteristics that humans possess. The living beings that are aware of its existence are aware of it thanks to the properties of their "brains". A program (artificial neural networks, machine learning, artificial intelligence, etc.) running on hardware designed from circuit elements made of known elements is not aware of its existence. (Naturally, it can be programmed in such a way that when it is asked "are you aware of your existence?" it can say "yes, I am aware". But the source of this is undoubtedly the technical team designing the hardware and software). When the structure of electronic circuit elements from living cells, which is currently in its infancy, develops, the relationship between electronics and living things - biomedical engineering - will go much further. However, in this case, as in previous examples, it is human-induced. Just as whatever exists (whether animate or inanimate matter or anything else cannot go beyond the characteristics that God/Allah has given them), the same is true for whatever has a human origin or structure (including such differences as a ship, train, airplane, etc. that goes faster than a human running, or a large number of multi-digit numbers that can be mathematically finalized in a very short period of time, etc., or a large amount of information that is stored in memory more than the living brain, etc.). Whatever the basis, "majority" has dominated in a multitude of meanings and structures for those living creatures and inanimate matter. However, while the natural course of things is going on, if a different voice "positively changes" the thinking of the majority in a way that they can understand, then it is possible to question the past in many ways. We can see that this has been done by many Great People in terms of shaping the history of the World. The relationship between living beings (of whatever species) will always and everywhere be different from the relationship that exists or will exist between living beings and whatever is a living product. This is even different from the relationship between a living being and inanimate matter. Whatever is known to "exist" and what is known to "not exist" by humans, if they produce the same effect in the brain (i.e., if the way they are perceived is the same), then both each human being can have a separate universe and the universe (concreteness) can be non-existent. The difference in the way each person's brain perceives things can be in the form of both the differentiation of the environment in which people live on a person-by-person basis (as it interacts with them) and the very rapid change or transformation of the environment as it affects each person. How can such a structure, which is in constant change in so many ways, "show such behavior?" The answers cannot fit into the memory of computers or the pages of books. However, what is referred to as the "environment" is the most general form of everything in every sense except God/Allah. This general structure has multifunctional and multivariable structures in the birth, development and death of everything. It is also created and is the greatest of the created. It knows everything it includes in it down to the finest detail, and even if the answer to the question "Whatever will occur in its interaction with them, will it produce results in its favor or in their favor?" is given as "in its favor", it can also be said to produce results "in favor of everything" in another sense because it includes/contains them (living beings). When the question is asked here, "how will the distribution be, that is, what will be the percentage of benefit of those involved?" it is at this very moment that social rules (pertaining to life and beyond) come into play. As is well known, these social rules can bring agreement and peace, but they can also bring war and conflict. Conflict can even reach such a level that a species can be completely wiped out. At even more advanced stages, a planet, etc. could also disappear. Going back to the topic mentioned at the beginning, was everything created by God/Allah (whatever was created - whether animate or inanimate matter - perceiving each other as if they existed in all kinds of communication with each other) within a structure or formation that in reality does not physically exist at all? Does this even explain all kinds of structures between them (in the scientific sense) in all sciences such as physics, chemistry, biology, mathematics, etc.? This is not to distort or misrepresent what exists, but to evaluate it in a different approach, in a purely intellectual sense. With this logic, if we now think that everything is made up of light and its compounds, and if we accept that this situation is different from the known and familiar light oil (i.e. that it has no particulate structure and is only made up of waves), then there will be a completely different approach in this sense. Since there is no physical or physical structure, everything can pass through each other. If it is said that there is a physical structure, it can be thought that they cannot pass through each other in a way that can be explained by an unknown science, and that this is perceived as such by living beings and the tools they design and build, whereas in reality this is not the case, but is perceived as such in the living brain (including on the basis of all tools and equipment). If this is the case, then concepts such as perception, sensation, etc. need to be better investigated, and engineering and medicine should engage in a different kind of research and effort together. (Although the concept of the soul comes to mind in this approach, this is not the situation that is intended to be explained.) It is intended to emphasize that this approach exists while the living or non-living object exists, and that this approach ends when it dies or disappears. (As mentioned above, it is clear that it is in no way overlapping or related to the concept of the soul.) Now, if this is the case, how can the "negativities" that exist between living beings and between living beings and inanimate matter, which should be the subject of fundamental investigation, be expressed in this sense and in this approach? Can "negativity" be completely "eliminated"? The answer to this question will be given by the level and development of science and technology. If it is to be eliminated, it would be more appropriate to reverse 180 degrees (in the sense of negativity effect) whatever causes negativity rather than changing the perception that occurs in the brain. Well, it may be a different approach to try to change their perceptions (i.e. the structure and situation that reaches them) rather than trying to change the negativity that exists between living beings and somehow negativity between them. It can be thought of as an

4

interface developed for electronic/electromechanical equipment using two (2) different communication methods (protocols) to communicate with each other. Here, it is not the person, but the change that the cause of negativity undergoes while reaching the target, that is, while moving through the transmission medium. An example of this is the transformation of an insulator into a conductor for the transmission of electric current, or vice versa, the transformation of the conductor into an insulator, rather than the destruction of the source of the current to prevent the current from being transmitted. While much progress has been made in the current (2024) years in all aspects of the content of thought, its structure from its source to its transmission and its destination, there is still much more to be studied, researched and solved. Just as it is not possible to understand nature in every sense - no matter what the scientific and technological level - the thought in the brain of living beings, which is a part and element of it, can be evaluated in the same logic. Even though science and technological progress bring solutions to many things, in parallel with progress, nature is changing its structure and this requires different scientific approaches to solve and understand this situation. Nature is completely alive and whatever is being done, what is happening, what is ending, etc., all happens within itself. Therefore, it (nature) develops and manifests a form of behavior accordingly. All of what we call "inanimate matter" in nature is in constant interaction with each other due to the many formations that exist in nature. Examples of these phenomena are wind, heat, light, soil, air, water, etc. and others. With the wind, a piece of stone can move and drop a fruit from a tree, and the kernel of the fallen fruit can cause a new fruit tree to grow there. These cannot be coincidences. They are phenomena that nature has developed and put into practice. If the operation of the hardware behind the random number generating code piece/section in a computer program is examined and monitored, it can be found what the number to be generated or obtained will be, that is, what value it will take.

The interaction of non-living substances among themselves can be understood to a certain extent with the sensors used. However, the result obtained here does not go further than the type, shape, state and structure of living things. This approach goes further than the internal structures of inanimate matter and the properties that living beings possess. It is not possible to comment on something/things that cannot be perceived. Because this situation is not within the scope of human limits. If it were, then there would be no distinction between living and non-living matter. In other words, if everything was alive or everything was inanimate matter, then there would be a difference. However, we see and understand by living that nature is not like that. This is expressed in "sentences". It is certain that this is not the case, so it is pointless to carry the situation further or beyond thought. On the contrary, it is more appropriate to think and evaluate every existing situation with multiple, multifunctional and multivariate thinking. This should be the ideal. On the other hand, when asked if the opposite can be realized, such environments can be created and the stages of thought can be practically achieved and seen. However, if one asks whether it can be abstracted from the general structure of nature, the answer is two (2). If it is created by living beings, it cannot be abstracted. If it is not created by living beings, then it is already abstract and is a phenomenon in the thoughts of living beings, waiting to be discovered. If both (two) states exist and there is communication between them, this situation extends to different dimensions. In other words, the bidirectional communication between what exists naturally and what is identical to nature is a situation that needs to be fully analyzed. In the continuation of these approaches, if we think that everything else except God/Allah is virtual, that is, that the only reality is that Almighty Creator, and that nothing other than Him actually comes from eternity and goes to eternity... Even God/Allah never needs anything else for which His own existence is sufficient. But His creatures that exist are nothing but His will.

That there is nothing other than His own existence coming from infinity and going to infinity, and that what exists is nothing other than what He has created. When thought in this way, He can create something that does not exist, and He can destroy it completely or temporarily at will. Again, in this approach, a conclusion can be drawn as follows: that even the volume occupied by its structure, which comes from eternity and progresses as such, is created by itself. At the very beginning (when we came from infinity) there was no volume that contained or did not contain anything. But God/Allah then created a volume for Himself first, and then created volumes (universes and the region between universes) for the living and non- living things He would create. In other words, God/Allah did not need anything in the first place. (In fact, He did not need any volume for His own existence.) In this case, both what is (His creations) and what is not could go to any coordinates at any time and exist there without going there. (An example of this approach is teleportation, which is the subject of study by scientists today, but which still has a long way to go. However, while teleportation here is the transportation of a substance to be teleported from one coordinates to another coordinates, it is a very different concept from its destruction and reappearance at the target location. In other words, there is transportation or teleportation within an existing volume. Whereas what belongs to God/Allah, as stated above, is to reach the desired target coordinates region there, whether it is an existing volume or not. In this sense, it is a very different formation from what His creations want to do or apply). When we think, "What was created first?" (beyond all the living and non-living things we know, perhaps billions of years, perhaps trillions, perhaps quadrillions, or much, much beyond), this is an ambiguous question, or one with no definite answer. Almighty God/Allah, who needs nothing and can create or destroy anything at will, may have created all of His creations in a "virtual" way, as we see ourselves in the mirror, so that there is nothing but Him. The source of this virtuality could have been something with an infinite number of colors. This could have been the background of all that is physically known and whose validity is not disputed. Thus, it seems more logical that if the "main source" in question is deactivated by God/Allah, the known "Apocalypse" will take place for everything created. In today's science and technology, there are many theories for the formation of the universe and universes. The light that sets out starting from the "main source" mentioned above may be both creating the volume in which it will progress and be effective and initiating the formation of the universe or universes in these volumes due to its structure, that is, its components. If this "Main Source" is considered with this logic, it means that there is nothing that its structure or content cannot create. There is also the fact that in the background of whatever is formed, there is a master set that encompasses it all. The question "Can there be any exit from this structure?" is very different from being a definite "yes" or "no". Because there are certainly other Creatures who experience concepts and values that are much different from the "yes" and "no" concepts that mostly known living beings have. These can only be approached on an intellectual basis. Countless parallel universes were formed from the structure of one and only one of the countless beams of rays emanating from the "Mother Source". There was an interaction between two of these universes that was beyond imagination. It was like the situation of two living beings who are either very close friends or very bitter enemies. The universes were named A and B. Universe A was formed earlier than universe B, and its volume was larger than the other. However, the logic of "the larger the volume, the more efficient", which is common among living things, did not apply to these two universes. The volume of universe B was approximately 1/1000000 of the volume of universe A. However, its content (in terms of application) was much higher than that of universe A. Also, in both universes, there was no living or non-living matter in any known sense. These two universes (A and B) were the first two universes to form. And trillions of years after their formation, other universes began to form. - So nothing else had happened or was going on other than the bickering between universes A and B for many, many years. - This bickering was the same as what the use of the phrase "it's in their genes" describes. They were opposite universes in every sense. The most obvious of these meanings was like the logic of the plus and minus poles of a battery. But this structure was much more than magnets with different poles attracting each other. They were not attracting each other, but repelling each other - like two people who don't want to see each other's faces. - Universe B was smaller, but it was more effective than Universe A in terms of repulsion or repulsion. In both universes, the light beams coming from their own formation and structure were effective in every sense. Within the two almost spherical universes, there were beams of light that moved randomly and did not terminate, that is, did not lose their effect. These beams of light were exerting pressure on the boundaries of the universe they were in from the inside, but this pressure did not cause the universe to expand, it caused whatever was outside the universe to go further. This was due to the different structures of the light beams, the different structures of the boundaries of the universes, and the structure of the region between universes. Also, some of the light beams (very, very small percentages) crossed the boundary through the internal structure of the universes and went out. When the boundary was crossed and the interstellar region was crossed, the light completely lost its known properties. This change was like a fluid turning into a solid. Thus, in the inter-universe region, structures similar to the familiar "suspension bridges" with no clear beginning and end appeared, albeit very rarely. But there was no such thing as a "suspension bridge" connecting the two universes (A and B) or allowing the transition from one to the other. There was a bridge between the two universes, but it was not a physical bridge as we know it. It was a bridge of feeling or thought. This was "pushing or sending each other as far away as possible". But over time, it seemed as if this non-physical state was turning into a tangible structure. There were no living beings in the universes, but the beams of light that were in constant motion within them were, in another sense, a different kind of life. Because they knew what they were doing and their purpose was clear. They even knew the path they had to follow to achieve it. But an impartial observer looking at these two universes from the outside would immediately recognize that Universe B was more intelligent. In fact, in this sense, some of the beams of light in both universes, some of those in A, were looking for ways to cross over to universe B and collapse them from within. In a way, this was no different from the logic of sending spies from one universe to another. The structure of the borders of Universe B is very strong, so there is no entry from the outside. If we consider the related phenomenon of displacement or coordinate change, we can reach the same (similar) conclusions. The situation that is not actually on/ between or within physical objects, but is in fact nothing but virtuality (a structure or formation that is another form of what is seen in dreams) may have been the case here as it is in the lives of all living beings (including humans). This was "pushing or sending each other as far away as possible". But over time, it seemed as if this non-physical state was turning into a tangible structure. There were no living beings in the universes, but the beams of light that were in constant motion within them were, in another sense, a different kind of life. Because they knew what they were doing and their purpose was clear. They even knew the path they had to follow to achieve it. But an impartial observer looking at these two universes from the outside would immediately recognize that Universe B was more intelligent. In fact, in this sense, some of the beams of light in both universes, some of those in A, were looking for ways to cross over to universe B and collapse them from within. In a way, this was no different from the logic of sending spies from one universe to another. The structure of the borders of Universe B is very strong, so there is no entry from the outside. If we consider the related phenomenon of displacement or coordinate change, we can reach the same (similar) conclusions. The situation that is not actually on/between or within physical objects, but is in fact nothing but virtuality (a structure or formation that is another form of what is seen in dreams) may have been the case here as it is in the lives of all living beings (including humans). In addition, the perception of the distance between the coordinates may have been the time it took for the light of these concepts to reach the relevant perception region of the brain or the time it took until it was perceived by the formation occurring within the brain itself. It could also have been the sum of the times valid for both. In this case, the following question should not be overlooked: when the situation in question is not perceived by a creature belonging to any species, is the situation in this creature an exact reflection of reality, or is there a problem with the creature? (The answer to this is known and is mostly valid for whatever decision/decisions are made or taken by the majority). We can see that sometimes there are various conflicts in this sense in every society. As a result, either a person who is different from the majority becomes dominant or the society, the majority, becomes dominant and can neutralize the person who is different in itself and in any way. (In general, when we look at the known history, we can see which of these situations is more effective depending on the conditions of the time.) Naturally, the conditions that are meant to be mentioned here can be explained as "differing from society to society". But in the case of a traveler (if he is in different societies at different times), he may naturally experience many contradictions. This contradiction may even be vital. If it is not vital, for example, a person's hand going from hot water to cold water, drinking water after choking on food, eating something very bitter after eating something very sweet, laughing and suddenly crying, clear skies and suddenly darkness, and so on. However, if this "traveler" interprets these as some of the necessities or naturalness of life, then this person is a prime candidate to become a leader both for the society in which he/she lives and for the celestial body in which societies live. If there were only one country on a celestial body, then the above-mentioned evaluations would be different. But we know that this is not the case, at least for the Earth. It contains many countries. When we consider these years (20XX), globalization, which started much earlier, continues at full speed both with constant and increasing momentum. Regardless of the areas of difference, there are common, unifying values. There are many values affecting the life of living beings that are now slowly being felt (but have been experienced and felt in many different parts of the world for a long time). Immediate examples of these are water problems, climate, food supply, health problems, extraterrestrial threats (although this is a matter of debate), and so on. Any living creature of any species can stand against these negativities up to a certain point or limit. The level of this resistance is directly proportional to the physical endurance of the creature in question and its ability to use its intellectual values. Currently, there is a large amount of stored information in digital media, including analog media. However, there are also shortcomings in general terms. The most important of them is this (and this is vital - not only for humans but also for other kinds of living beings): It is practically not enough to record or store all the thoughts of every human being from the moment he or she is born (or even before he or she is born), at least in terms of the medium for recording (if it can be achieved) - in terms of capacity. There are also fundamental problems (in a scientific and technological sense.) Because a human being can have a wide variety of thoughts at any moment, while walking, running, resting, eating, studying, etc. The ability to record them at any moment is a technological problem in itself. What is currently known is that only in certain environments - private - these recording processes can be done with specialized hardware. This situation or approach brings with it the need for further scientific and technological development. If it can be achieved one day in the future, then (if it does not cause problems in a special sense - with legal regulations) many negative phenomena that are currently a problem or may cause problems will be eliminated. Even if this does not happen, its negative impact will be minimized. The most important of these will be the elimination of the negativities that apply to society in general (regardless of the country). When we look at history, there are many people whose thoughts have guided (positively or negatively) a very large region, starting with the society in which they live. Naturally, some of them were considered "positive" for everyone, while others were considered "positive" or negative only for some. We can also see that the concepts of "positive" and "negative" are interchangeable in different time periods. In other words, there are some people who were previously considered "heroes" (in the time period in which they lived) and were later referred to as the opposite, or who were first seen as "negative" and later considered "heroes". This is more often the case for people who wanted to or did contribute, rightly or wrongly, to the "scientific and technological" process. In military terms, the situation is very different. The saviors of nations were considered "heroes" for that nation, but "obstacles because they could not do what they could do" for the nations that wanted to dominate that nation. There is no one person on a celestial body who is considered "positive" by all the people living there. Even if they are considered "positive" by everyone, they are considered the opposite of "positive" for at least one person. This includes the Prophets, the Great Messengers of God/Allah. We can see this very clearly from the perspectives of those who accept the religions that exist and live in the world today. This is even why "wars" are taking place in the world today. If thoughts from the first moment of humanity's existence had been recorded on a medium in any way (Today, this recording medium is magnetic media and additionally DNA.) However, when considered in terms of capacity, a different recording technology than today's technology is required for the entirety of every human being's thoughts in the smallest period of time. Space and its continuation, the universe, is the best medium for recording information of any kind in any form. Both in terms of capacity and other characteristics. However, as is known, the universe is open to the formation and development of all kinds of matter, known and unknown. This includes everything from the most solid matter to the softest matter. If information can be recorded especially in the so-called "space", then there will be no such concepts as lack of memory or lack of capacity. The following logic or approach can be followed here: What will be stored as the equivalent of the value to be recorded? Is it a gas, a solid, a liquid or some other form of matter, or is it dark matter or dark energy, which is said to dominate most of the universe at present? This question must be answered. Current technology does not go beyond electrical quantities or anything else. If a structure can be implemented that affects and changes the distribution of whatever or whatever is in the environment in question, then there is no need to search for an answer to what can be used instead of the information to be recorded. Because there are already ready-made components in the environment. If their coordinates can be changed without changing until a new recording, then the problem in question will be solved by itself. However, in this approach, there are naturally different components in the existing universe regions. There are some other problems, such as how it can be applied to different components, or whether the logic of this approach can be used for each component. If the same application can be realized for whatever is unsuitable and dangerous for living things, especially for humans, then both the dangerous substance in question will be used for a purpose of living things and the danger will be eliminated or controlled. There are many phenomena that pose a danger in this sense for today's people. Some of these can be fully or partially controlled with today's technology, and there are some that cannot be controlled at all. However, with evaluation and solution approaches in the numerical environment, inputs and outputs can be monitored and evaluated and the relationship between them can be expressed in mathematical terms. (With linear or nonlinear systems of equations.) The "nonlinear" approach in question here can be linked to the concept or approach of "random number generation" in software. Because there is a range in which both can take values. Even if these limits are minus infinity and plus infinity. One could also ask the question of writing whatever one wants to save to sequential memory, which is the known approach, and if there is no space after a certain stage, continuing to write from another free region. This approach may not be used. So there is information, but the smallest unit of information can be written to random memory regions. In this case, it is naturally necessary to know the address where that information is stored. In another sense, this can be expressed in a formation or approach such as a "file access table". If the information is stored in this way, both the writing time and the time to read this information will be much, much longer than in a sequential approach. (For example, if information/information on Earth is not recorded in very distant regions of the universe - excluding other star systems, other universes, etc. - there will be no or negligible loss in terms of speed or time. - In terms of the perception and evaluation time of living beings and humans. - Since everything depends on, or is evaluated as, the change or whatever that occurs in the region of the brain affected by the signal, it is open to everything on the basis of "interpretation". The perception in question can be evaluated as something "concrete" or, on the contrary, as an "abstract" formation. However, there is a fundamental difference between the created beings, which is that (relative to each other) one is alive, i.e. aware of its existence, and the other is inanimate, i.e. not aware of its existence. However, inanimate matter and the living product can be related in many things. For example, a computer program is also not aware of its existence. In this case, the hardware and software components called "artificial intelligence" can be considered in the same class and it can be said that they are "inanimate matter". However, if a formation can be obtained or realized using these components from living cells that we know, then the "artificial intelligence" in question - "becomes aware of its existence". In this sense, it would be a "living" being in the sense that it would be evaluated by living beings - especially humans. At this moment, there may be many conflicts or contradictions with living beings. There has never been and will never be non- existence in any sense and at any time. God/Allah always exists. This shows the continuity of "existence" from the lowest to the highest level (in terms of created beings), even if there is at least one. Rather than questioning creation in every sense, it would be a better approach to try to understand, formulate, explain, etc. the communication of the created beings (whether living, non-living matter or something else) among themselves in every meaning and structure in the broadest dimensions. In this way, life will gain meaning and value, instead of just waiting for it to pass. All that exists (all that has been created) is in constant interaction, whether it is understood by them or not. This interaction can be positive or negative. Which of these situations will occur depends on many reasons. Anyone who has not been raised well, starting from the family he/she was born into, who has not gained positivity in the process of education and training (science, morality, religion, health, sports, fine arts, etc.) will interact negatively with his/her environment in every sense. On the other hand, individuals who have positively acquired the above-mentioned conditions will naturally interact positively with their environment. Now let's imagine that only one person from each of these 2 (two) structures is alone on a planet. There are no other people on the planet, but there are animals of all kinds and many of all kinds of structures. These 2 (two) people continue to live on the same planet for many years, unaware of each other's existence. While living like this, one day, somehow, by chance, they come across each other. Both of them have limited technology, whatever they use. For example, neither of them should have any electronic devices. The positive person realizes that the negative person in front of him is missing some of the objects he is carrying and gives him a certain number of the ones he has. (Let's assume that both people were born on this planet and their families left later.) Whether positive or negative, every living being respects their parents in very high percentages. When they are away from them for a certain period of time, they miss them and want to see them. Thus, these 2 (two) people meet at a common point (intersection cluster) with the longing for "mother and father" despite their diametrically opposed approaches to their environment. We accept that they both speak the same language. They will immediately start tracing their parents. While searching the planet for this purpose, they find a note written by their parents in a cave before they left the planet. Both of their parents have left separate notes. These notes should read: "We went to another habitable planet in a spaceship. We left you here on purpose and on purpose. So we expect you to start from scratch in everything on your own and control and manage yourself in every sense. In addition, we have left a lot of information in terms of - space sciences. We want you to use them to build a spaceship, even a small one, and come to the planet whose coordinates we have given you with the spaceship you will build. We built such a spaceship ourselves in ten (10) years before you both were born. We deliberately and intentionally hid this from you because we did not want to give you a copy that adds value and meaning to life. Also, we did not have any resources when we built the spaceship. We started everything from scratch with 4 (four) people. Now we expect at least the same work or even more from you. The sooner you complete the spaceship and make it operable, the sooner you will reach us. Start working now. Each of you was 15 (fifteen) years old when we left you. We were on average 40-45 years old when we left that planet, because we were not all the same age." They read this note both positively and negatively. They had found it by chance in a cave they had accidentally entered about 1.5 years after their parents had left the planet. They also could not make sense of the fact that they had left the note not in the cave where they had lived with their parents before, but in a very different, even very distant cave. However, after reading the note, when they turned the back side of the almost A1-sized paper, they saw the sketch of the cave they were in at that moment. With the paper in their hands and looking at it, they walked about 200 meters further into the cave and came across an elevator that, as they could see from the sketch, went down underground. When they reached the bottom of the elevator door, it opened. Both of them entered without waiting. At that very moment, an electromechanical robot came to them. It told them briefly why it had come and for what purpose it would help them. "Then you will help us build a spaceship too, won't you?" they asked positively and negatively. And the robot said "yes, that is my main and primary duty to you. You have hit the nail on the head". While these conversations were going on, about 5 (five) minutes had passed. On the numerical displays in the elevator, there was information that "they were 2 (two) kilometers deeper than the point they had boarded". Negative asked the robot "why are we going so deep, are we going to continue?". The robot replied, "It will take another 5 (five) minutes. So we will go approximately 5 (five) kilometers deeper than the point where you get into the elevator. There is a very large horizontal section there. It's a huge unit suitable for building all kinds of equipment and devices - including spaceships. There are many robots in it, many robots that can do many, many different tasks, to help you build a spaceship." Another five minutes came and went and the elevator stopped. Then the robot stayed in the elevator while they both stepped out. After their exit, another robot came to them this time. This robot also told them why and why not, and together they began to walk around the horizontal unit that the first robot had mentioned. The first thing they saw and noticed, both positive and negative, were thousands of robots, even more industrious than ants. Some of the robots were carrying things and some were doing things. They wondered, "What is this robot doing?" So the affirmative and the negative with the robot next to them walked up to a robot that was working at that moment and looked at what it was doing. The robot in question was sitting in an armchair, looking at the books on a rather large table and looking at the computer screen on the table, writing and drawing on the white paper in front of him. Positive's curiosity got the better of him and he asked, "Can I find out what it is doing?" The robot first raised a finger on one hand and said "one minute". Then it put down the different pencil next to the paper and turned to them and said, "I am doing research and development for a new spaceship engine. We are working on an engine that is very different from the engine of the spaceship your parents went on. I am just one of the robots working on it. Exactly 300 (three hundred) robots are working on this subject. Our president is also a robot like us. We give our work to him in certain periods and he checks and informs us about how our work will continue." Then he added: "We will take you both to an education and training camp that will last exactly 7 (seven) years. At the end of this period you will have - as the old Earthers say - three professions - computer, aircraft, automation and control engineering. So in about 10-12 years, you will have completed the spaceship of our own design, which we robots will help you assemble. And then you will be on your way to the planet where your parents are, to be reunited with them." Meanwhile, the negative: "can't I have the professions you just mentioned without going through the process of education and training?" The robot replied: "It is not possible to have something without doing anything, without working. So you want to go from one place to another. But not on foot, not by a vehicle, not by thinking. You say you want to go from where you are to where you want to go with zero effort. This is not a situation that is valid for any of the created beings. In fact, what you are saying is something even more advanced and beyond teleportation, and we don't even have teleportation technology." The positive robot listening to the conversation said to the positive robot: "I accept what you have said. It doesn't matter, I will work in his place. Because he wants to see his parents as much as we want to see our parents." Negative "Yes, I want to work too, but I prefer to work physically rather than in this sense. Because I am quite strong and I think you can help me a lot in transportation". Upon this, the robot said: "If you are thinking about transportation, then carry it, but we will ask one more thing from you. Would you like to work in the design and construction of the vehicles we will use for transportation?" Negative: "What would that be like?" Robot: "Drawing such vehicles using computer programs, running the vehicle in a simulator and then physically building it, etc. Is that OK?" Negative: "OK, it's just the job for me". Robot: "since we have agreed on the type of education and training, before we start the process, we will put you both through a preparation period, just like football players go through a training camp for a match." Positive: "will this process take place here or upstairs, outside the cave?" Robot: "I would expect you not to ask such a question, or if you do, I would expect you to answer it yourself". Positive: "why?" Robot: "There are many reasons why it cannot or should not be outside the cave. The most important of these reasons is already known to you. Because every day hundreds of meteors, big and small, come from space and hit our planet. So if we work outside the cave and a big one of these meteorites falls or hits there, our work will be wasted. Isn't it?" Affirmative: "yes you are right, I hadn't thought about that." Negative: "Well, are we going to stay here, kilometers below the surface, until the work is finished? We will never go up or out?" Robot: "That's not possible. We will go up in certain periods. But when we go up, we will not take even the smallest thing related to our work with us. Because in every sense this place is incomparable to up there and safer in every way". Negative: "What is the period you are talking about?" Robot: "I don't know right now, I need to ask our president robot who is responsible for the security here. Let's go to him if you want". Then both positive and negative accepted what the robot said. They left the point where they were to go to the president robot by getting on a vehicle that moves horizontally and looks just like a land vehicle. There were positive, negative and a robot in the vehicle. They traveled together and reached the place where the president robot was located after about 25 (twenty-five) minutes. Here, kilometers below the surface, there were no columns. It was a very large and flat structure, just like a plain or a plateau. There were different sections, but there were no walls or physical barriers between them. The only difference was that there were lighted signs with the name of each section and documents with the characteristics of the robots in charge there. Also, the president robot was almost 10 (ten) times taller than the other robots. Therefore, it also weighed more than them. The question previously asked by the negative to the other robot had reached the other robot through the electronic devices used. When the negative was preparing to ask the same question to the president robot, the answer he received was "yes, that period is 7 (seven) days". Then the president robot added: "There is such a section here that it is much more advanced than the natural state of the outside. I will take you there too. Maybe when you see it, you will never want to go up". Both positive and negative: "In any case, we would like to go outside once every seven (7) days." President Robot: "Wait, don't decide until you see the place I mentioned. I think you will not want to go out every 7 (seven) days, but maybe every 7 or 10 months." Thereupon, both positive and negative robots were eager to see the area that was the subject of the president's confident speech. They both said, "Well, let's go there right away, I wonder what's there." So they got back into the vehicle that brought them there, the positive, the negative, the robot president and the other robot, and set off on a journey that started all over again. This time the vehicle was going faster. Again, after a journey of about half an hour, they arrived at the area mentioned by the president robot. The president robot got out of the vehicle first, then the positive and negative robot, and finally the other robot. After they got off, they walked for about 150 meters and the positive and negative were shocked by what they encountered. Because just 20 (twenty) meters away from them was a huge screen on which they could see their parents' lives on the planet they had visited. They also had their voices along with the image. It must have been the longing of the positive and negative for their parents, because both of them started touching the screen with both hands as if they wanted to touch their parents on the screen. They both asked the robot president: "we see and hear them, do they see and hear us? If so, we would like to talk to our parents". To this question, the robot president said: "yes, just as you see and hear them, they see and hear you, and you can talk to each other". Negative immediately interjected, crying and saying "I miss you so much, why did you leave us and go away?". When the father of the negative was about to answer this question, the robot president immediately intervened and said "let me explain this". At this, the father of the negative said "okay". The robot president said: "Your species has such a characteristic. This feature has been given to you as a duty by God/Allah who created you. And it is this: When every new baby born to your species reaches a certain age, its parents leave it on the planet where it was born and leave that planet to go to another planet. And this is going on all the time. Is that clear?" Negative: "yes, I understand." The mother of both the positive and the negative said, "The sooner and more successfully you complete the spaceship, the sooner you will be with us." Negative: "and when we complete it and come to you, will we stay on the planet you are on now, or do we have to go back here again?" To this question - the president robot intervened - replied: "When you get there, you will not stay there. You will stay there for a little while and then you will come back here in the spaceship you went in." Negative: "how long will we be able to stay". President robot: "this time is also predetermined and decided. It can be a maximum of 7 (seven) days. More than that is unlikely. I would also like to point out that the first couple of your descendants, the two people who are generations and generations behind you, had the greatest wish: - May our lineage reach as many planets as it can reach. May our lineage spread to all the planets in our universe. Even further, if it is possible, to reach other universes and the planets in those universes. God/Allah created the universes and all that is in them, and the more of them we can reach, the closer we are to God/Allah - that's what I and the other robots are here to support and help you to fulfill this wish of your first two ancestors." Affirmative: "yes, we didn't know that, we just found out, so we should work to fulfill this wish of our ancestors, the beginning of our lineage." Negative: "yes, I agree." President robot: "we can start the preparation for your education and training process." Positive: "where and how long will this preparation process be." President robot: "the duration is 7 (seven) days, and the location is somewhere outside the planet we are currently on. You will go to a space station in orbit and the robots there will give you all kinds of support - like the ones here - on what to do." For better or for worse, this was the first time they were going off the planet. In that sense they were both very excited. Negative: "so when are we going to go to that space station?" President robot: "Everything is going on and will go on as planned. A robot friend of mine, who you see now and who is approaching us, will take you to the space station and take you to the spaceship." When the robot that approached them came to them, he said "let's go". Positively and negatively, they followed them on foot. After a walk of about 500 (five hundred) meters, they came to the section where the spaceship in question was located. Immediately after being detected by the sensors on the door when they approached, the door opened and the three of them entered the spaceship. The spaceship was not big. Besides themselves, there were two (2) other robots inside. In other words, there were a total of 2 (two) living beings (positive and negative) and 3 (three) robots in the spaceship. One of the robots inside said to the positive and negative: "You don't even need to sit anywhere. Because our journey to reach the space station will take at most 5 (five) minutes. However, if you prefer, you can sit in one of the seats you want." Positive: "If the journey will be short, then we would like to learn about the equipment on the spaceship instead of sitting down, wouldn't we, Negative?" Negative disagreed with Positive and said "I would like to sit down". The five minutes came and went like the blink of an eye. The spaceship landed on the space station. There were many living beings and robots in the space station. This space station did not belong to just one planet. It was the result of the collaborative efforts of many planets that contained living beings. And there were not just one (1) of them. . The number of celestial bodies in that universe that fit the dimensions of planets, and the number of living beings (human beings, animals, plants or any other kind of life...) were produced and orbited by the planets in question. However, the size and contents of each space station were not the same. This varied according to the characteristics of the planets they orbited. Each one contained many laboratories of different sciences. Those who came here for the first time, apart from their positive and negative parents, were seeing different living beings for the first time. In addition, these creatures did not resemble themselves in appearance at all. They were 10 cm tall, 2.5 m tall, blue, green, red, etc., with one eye, four arms, no ears, etc. Here, for 7 (seven) days, the positive and negative would be given information about planets and other universes other than their own. From all kinds of characteristics of the celestial bodies there to the inhabitants. The positive and negative were not small, but they were sometimes frightened by the creatures with different physical characteristics that they were seeing for the first time. However, as soon as such creatures began to communicate with them and provide information about their universe and their planet, the fear of the positive and negative gave way to curiosity about what they were listening to and what they were about to hear. They were both taken to the conference room of the space station. Here they were to be presented with information about the different universes and planets from which the creatures on the space station had come. This presentation would not be on a screen, but in a more advanced application of hologram technology, a technology that is still in use today. The area allocated for this purpose was approximately 1,000 square meters. Near the presentation area, positive and negative people sat down to watch the presentation, which would last for 3.5 to 4 hours. The presentation started immediately. From the moment it started, they began to feel as if they were on a journey between universes and planets. Whatever they had seen and heard in the presentation, they were encountering for the first time. Therefore, the presentation was very important and valuable, especially in terms of the information they would acquire. In fact, during the presentation, depending on the situation, creatures with different characteristics living on the planets would come to where the positive and negative were sitting and speak to them in a language they would understand. This practice in the presentation - that is, different living beings speaking to them - both excited and delighted the positive and the negative. Sometimes they were even very scared and excited because of the fireball-shaped large and small celestial bodies coming towards them during the presentation - they were afraid that they would be hit by them. But this fear was unwarranted, because everything was nothing different from the digital images. There was also an interesting phenomenon, which they liked very much. They traveled in the sense of a hologram inside the "black holes" formed when stars complete their lives. At these moments, a darkness called pitch black dominated the whole environment. In this way, the minutes were passing one after the other. The presentation was completed and a living being approached them: "Now we are going to take you on a 2 (two) hour space journey in a spaceship different from the spaceship you came here in. So you will be able to see different celestial bodies from the planet you live on." Thereupon, the negative: "Will we be able to see the planet where our parents are, will we be able to go there too?" Live: "No, that is not included. You know that you will go there with your own spaceship that you will realize with the work you will do." Negative: "ok". Immediately after the end of the presentation, the positive and negative were taken into the spaceship, which was already ready, and the spaceship started traveling. The spaceship would travel at very high speeds. Thus, they would be able to see more and different celestial bodies, both positive and negative. Within this 2 (two) hour travel time, they would have traveled around a region as far as reaching the outside of today's Milky Way Galaxy. Apart from the positive and negative, there were no other living beings on the spaceship. But there were a certain number of robots. As the ship traveled at high speed, its speed gradually began to decrease and eventually the ship stopped. The positive and negative inside the spaceship could not understand what was happening, but when they looked through the transparent part of the ship through which they could see outside, they saw a structure with a blinding white glow that completely covered them. This was nothing more than a virtual exercise to "test" the positive and negative inside the ship. They were both very frightened and said to themselves, "I guess we won't be able to get out of here and we won't be able to see our parents". They stayed like this, that is, stuck where they were, for about 10 (ten) minutes. However, after this time, the celestial body surrounding the spaceship disappeared and the spaceship continued its journey. Thus, after they had gotten rid of their positive and negative fears, a robot came right up to them and explained to both of them the situation that had just occurred. In other words, "the situation was not real, it was virtual and it was meant to test them".

Although both positive and negative were a little angry, they didn't go any further and asked why they hadn't been told beforehand that they were going to face such a situation. However, the answer they received was enough for them. Finally, the 2 (two) hours of travel time was completed and the spaceship returned to the space station. After completing the time they had to stay in the space station, they were going to take the spaceship that brought them to the station back to their planet, that is, to the depths of that cave, by elevator and continue their work. - The years in which all these events took place were years that can be expressed in 1XX.XXXs according to the Earth year (X=0,1,2...9) and they took place in the universe in which the Earth is located. In particular, the positive was working on the intellectual side, in the sense of building a spaceship, while the negative was working on the physical side, in the sense of building a spaceship (as they had previously agreed and agreed upon). The robots' request from Positive was to design a spaceship that would have a physical shape that was unknown until that moment. While thinking about this, Positive started his engineering education, which would make him have 3 (three) different professions. In parallel with the education and training process, the creation of the outer appearance of the spaceship continued in parallel. He was examining all the shapes in positive geometry and doing an intensive intellectual and visual study on "how can I find a different and so far unknown geometric shape both using and not using them?". He was constantly increasing his technical knowledge with the training he had received and was receiving. Positively, he was engaged in a very intense work of finding "different geometric shapes". Not only the time he allocated for this purpose, but also when he was walking on the road, when he lay down on the bed, he was constantly thinking about it until he fell asleep. In fact, this thought had become so ingrained and prominent in him that even in his dreams he would see himself "working" on it. Sometimes, however, the shape that was different from other known shapes would appear in his mind, but only for a very, very short period of time, and before he had time to make sense of it and draw or record it in any way on a medium, the shape would fly away and disappear in his revived mind. He concentrated on this subject additionally. He asked one of the robots around him, "Is it possible to record everything that appears in my mind on an electronic medium?" The answer he got from the robot was "yes, of course it is possible". Positive: "so what do we need to do for that?" Robot: "We will place a piece of electronic equipment much smaller than a pico cubic meter on the top of your head. In this way, whatever you think about will be transmitted by electromagnetic waves to a receiver that will digitally record this information in the computer's memory". Positive: "will this hardware have any negative health effects on me?" The robot replied: "no, no, there is absolutely no such thing. You will not even feel the point where it touches your head in any way. Because that's how that tiny hardware is." Positive: "Well, then put it on my head." Robot: "ok, come with me, a biomedical doctor will position that hardware on your head." Walking along with the robot, the positive immediately reached the section close to the working section. The doctor here asked the positive to sit on the seat he showed. Positive sat down and in about 1 (one) minute, the electronic equipment was fixed on the top of the positive's head at a point that would be in contact with his/her head. Afterwards, the positive person got up from the seat and left that section with the robot. They reached the main work area again. Thus, while the positive was "consciously" engaged in the work he was doing and would do, on the other hand, his work on the subject that he was not aware of at all or partially unaware of was being recorded for later examination through that hardware in his head. He set a deadline for this and decided on 24 (twenty-four) hours. In other words, within this period of time, he was doing an intensive and exhausting work to combine both his own work and the intellectual information stored in the computer memory and blend them all together to obtain a different and hitherto unknown geometric shape, and he would continue his work until he found it. Thus minutes, hours, days, weeks, weeks, months and years passed by. Finally, the education and training process was over and so was the work. All the work on the spaceship was finished and the ship was being assembled. Positive could not find a different geometric shape, but the spaceship was transformed into a physical structure that would contain the maximum number of dimensions in the region of coordinates through which the spaceship passed. In other words, if there were 3 (three) dimensions where the spaceship passed through, the ship would turn into three dimensions, if there were 7 (seven) dimensions, it would turn into a physical shape of seven dimensions and so on. In another sense, this was a formation that could be considered as the dimensions taking different geometric shapes relative to each other. In a period of three to four months, the spaceship was completely ready. Over the years, they had left behind their youth, both positive and negative, and had reached what is called the middle age group. In the same way, their longing for their parents had reached its peak. Even though they were having a video chat with their parents on the screen in the depths of the cave, it was a far cry from talking and seeing each other in person. Now everything was ready. They talked to their parents on the screen, both positive and negative, and told them that the spaceship was ready and it was time to come to them. The exact coordinates of the planet were learned based on information from their parents' planet. On the spaceship that was going to go there, the positive, negative, 2 (two) robots and 1 (one) parakeet, one of his mother's favorite animals, and 1 (one) rabbit, one of his father's favorite animals, were to be taken there. According to the calculations, the journey would take about 2 (two) months. The basic necessities and other things that would be needed during this time were placed in the relevant sections of the spaceship. In addition, everyone on the spaceship (except two

(2) robots) were going to a different planet than their own for the first time. They were excited not because they were going on a positive or negative journey, but because they were going to see their parents again after many years. The parakeet and rabbit on board were out of their natural habitat for the first time. The spaceship was brought to the surface from the depths of the cave with the help of another elevator. Then the final checks were made and the ship took off slowly from its base, then increased its speed linearly and set off for the target planet. Thus began the 2 (two) month journey. In accordance with the work done by the positive before, the spaceship was moving through the universe it was in. As it was passing through different galaxies, the different number of dimensions that the galaxies in question had due to their different characteristics were reflected on the spaceship in the same way, and the ship transformed its normal 3 (three) dimensions into different dimensions. Although they were in the same universe, different galaxies could have different dimensions. However, the change in the total number of dimensions was not something that happened very often, even in different galaxies. Until that moment, the spaceship had set out with a 3 (three) dimensional structure, but due to the different dimensional structure in the different galaxies it passed through, it was faced with a change up to a maximum of 7 (seven) dimensions. Moreover, this increase or change was not sequential. For example, while there were 3 (three) dimensions in one galaxy, there could be 5 (five) dimensions in another galaxy, 7 (seven) dimensions in another, and so on. Even the dimensions of 2 (two) neighboring galaxies could be very different from each other. One could have 3 (three) dimensions, while the one next to it could have 7 (seven) dimensions. While the spaceship was undergoing a dimensional change in terms of its outer hull, there was no change in the dimensions of its occupants and they maintained their normal dimensions. The end of the journey was approaching. They could see the planet their parents were on through the receiver on the spaceship,

both positive and negative, in a structure where the image was getting bigger and clearer. In the meantime, their parents had given them a nasty surprise and cut off their electronic communication link with the positive and negative. The reason for this was that they were saying among themselves, "they will be here in a few hours anyway, let them miss us so that we can meet them". When the spacecraft entered the legal boundaries of the target planet, another spacecraft arrived to escort it and guide it. The spaceship of the positive and the spaceship of the negative, with the guiding ship in the lead, landed at the landing base on the target planet. Their parents had been waiting there almost 5-6 hours before the spaceship bringing their children landed at the base. After the landing, two (2) robots came out first. Then the positive and the negative. The negative had a parakeet in a wooden cage, while the positive had a rabbit in a wooden box. As soon as they stepped out of the spaceship, both of them immediately met their parents. They were all very different from the last time they had seen them alive. Their children had grown up and they themselves had aged a little bit. So both the positive and the negative and their parents were very happy. But the negative had a plan that he had been thinking about for a long time and wanted to realize, and that was this: the ship had landed at the base on the planet. He wanted to go back to the ship in the middle of the night without being seen by anyone, go inside and turn on the self-destruct mode of the ship. The ship would then self-destruct in about ten (10) minutes. Negative's main thought in this plan was to stay with his parents and not be separated from them anymore. He started to implement his plan and put the ship into "self-destruct" mode. About 10 (ten) minutes after he stepped out of the ship, the ship self-destructed. This self-destruction was completed in a different way from the usual sense of the ship being blown up or destroyed by a bomb. Within ten minutes, the ship began to melt rapidly and the melted metal flowed around like mercury and water and mixed with the soil of that planet.

Then the negative went to the positive and explained the situation, as if he hadn't done it himself. When Positive and the other 2 (two) robots arrived, they saw that the ship was no longer in place and that it had melted and mixed with the surrounding natural structure. Positive said: "How can this happen, the artificial intelligence on the ship did not put the ship in this state for no reason. Either it encountered a danger we don't know about or someone did it on purpose." However, just like the "black box" in airplanes, the logic and structure was valid for this spaceship. The black box-like hardware had remained unmelted and was standing where the ship was. He had forgotten or did not know this when he realized his negative thought before. The black box-like hardware was immediately examined and it was learned that the negative had clearly put the ship into "self- destruct" mode. After some back and forth conversations, the negative was in a difficult situation and confessed and admitted his crime. When asked why, he said that he did it because "he didn't want to be separated from his parents anymore". However, this negativity of the negative was not something that would go further or beyond destroying a spaceship. Because after the completion of their stay here, a spaceship from the planet they came from would take the two (2) of them and the two (2) robots back to their planet. After this situation was explained to the negative in all clarity, the negative started running to the nearest forest on the planet with dense trees and many forests so as not to return to the planet they came from and so that they would not find him. He wanted to lose track of himself in the dense woods and prevent anyone from finding him and taking him back to the planet they came from. After twenty minutes of running, he reached the dense forest. There were many wild poisonous weeds and thorns in the forest. There were also wild animals. He saw and realized this just a minute or two after he entered the forest. The shoes on his feet were sturdy and durable, but the pants he was wearing were made of cloth and the hem was torn in places because he had tripped over thorns while taking steps. The thorns scratched, wounded and bled his ankles. When poisonous weeds were applied to these wounds and came into contact with them, he soon fainted and fell where he was before he could move further into the forested area. He had been unconscious for about 2 (two) hours when an orangutan passing by noticed the situation and took him in his arms and took him to where he was staying in a tall tree with a wide and thick trunk. The negative was still unconscious and the orangutan took pieces of grass and trees and pressed them against the negative's wound, which was still bleeding, and then wrapped them around the wound and tied them with vines. This was probably a form and method of treatment that the orangutans knew about. After lying unconscious in this way for exactly 2 (two) days, he was shocked when he came to his senses. As he was about to faint again from the shock, the orangutan was trying to get him to drink fruit juice in an object resembling a large walnut shell. The negative was so thirsty that he didn't think whether it was water or something else, and he started to drink more and more because he was so thirsty. He drank 6 (six) full shells of the juice in that shell. After a short time, he came to himself a little and looked around. Immediately he realized the situation. That is, after he fainted, he realized that an orangutan had brought him to this place in this tree and healed him. After 1 (one) day in the tree, he came to his senses and realized that he had recovered, although he was not as strong as before. Next to him, many orangutans were constantly watching him. They too noticed the positive change in the negative. After a short while, the large orangutan that had brought him there again grabbed the negative with one arm and with the other arm, grabbing the relevant parts of the tree, lowered the negative down from the tree. The tree was so high that it was as tall as today's 60 (sixty) story skyscrapers. Looking up from under the tree, the negative began to walk through the woods without being able to see his saviors because they were too high up and there were too many branches and leaves on the tree. This time he plucked some thick, tough and wide grasses and tied them tightly with vines to cover the area from the top of his shoes up to his kneecaps. In this way, he was able to protect or secure the area below the kneecaps against thorns and poisonous weeds. It was a little difficult for him to walk this way, but there was nothing else he could do or knew of. In the woods, there was no problem of eating or drinking. Because there were many fruits both on the ground and on the trees, he plucked as many as he wanted and washed, cleaned and ate them with the water that gushed up from the ground through the grass at frequent intervals. When he was thirsty, he drank as much clean water as he wanted. As he walked through the forest, he thought that he had lost his trail and that no one would find him. But he had forgotten one thing. He had forgotten about the electronic hardware that was installed inside his skull at the moment he was born, which enabled him to be tracked/understand where he was going etc. This hardware inside the skull was constantly sending the coordinates of the negative via electromagnetic waves to the receivers in both the positive and the other 2 (two) robots. Thus, the location of the negative was known by the positive and the other 2 (two) robots as if it were in the palm of their hands. The situation here was also understood on the planet they came from. Both the destruction of the spaceship and the knowledge that the negative had escaped. The two robots entered the woods to catch the negative. Meanwhile, a spaceship from the planet they had come from was on its way here with a large number of robots on board. The ship would arrive here in about 2.5 (two and a half) months. As the robots moved through the forest, they were constantly aware of the coordinates of the Negative, so they came to the bedside of the Negative who was sleeping under a tree. The Negative was awakened by the sound of the branches on the ground where the robots had stepped while walking, and realizing that he was wanted and about to be caught, he quickly got up and started running away from where he was. Behind him, the robots were running at the same speed. Finally, he got tired and stopped near a tree. The robots were right next to it. Negative took one of the thick and long dry branches that had fallen to the bottom of the trunk of the tree and started to hit the 2 (two) robots standing next to him randomly and very strongly. The robots could not react to this sudden situation. Therefore, their mechanical and electronic components were damaged by the violent blows of the branches. Some parts were broken, some were damaged and some electronic components were short-circuited due to the impact. The fire, which started as a small spark with the flame caused by the short circuit, gradually grew and spread in the forest area. The flames and smoke were now visible from far, far away. Realizing the seriousness of the situation, the negative immediately started running out of the forest area. However, while running uncontrollably, his foot caught on one of the vines on the ground and he fell face down on the ground. His head hit one of the branches violently and he fainted for the second time. It did not take much time for the flames to reach the negative lying unconscious on the ground. Meanwhile, those of the animals in the forest that were able to escape began to flee and fly out of the forest area. But the same was not true for the negative. While he was unconscious, he started to burn in the flames that covered and engulfed him and he died in a very terrible way. The fire continued for about 2 (two) months. Because the forest area was very big. When the fire was over, the spaceship had arrived here. Since the electronic equipment in the negative's skull was not damaged, the robots that came with the spaceship and the negative's parents reached the location of the negative's lifeless body in a short time. The parents and the robots standing next to them saw the charred body of the Negative on the ground. The parents were shocked to see their son like this. Immediately they were both quickly taken by robots to the spaceship to be treated. The Negative's body was also taken and buried somewhere there after a religious ceremony.

This burial took place before the negative's parents had recovered from their shock. Within two days they had recovered from the shock to a certain extent. As for the positive, who had been living it all along, his eyelids were swollen and his eyes were red from crying. The spaceship that had just arrived on that planet took the positive person and the two (2) robots that the positive person had rendered dysfunctional before his death. The positive's eyes needed to be treated as soon as possible. Some therapeutic interventions had been made on the ship they were on at that moment, but they were not fully adequate and sufficient. Aware of the situation inside the spaceship, it reached the planet about 2 weeks earlier than the normal transportation time. The Positive was taken deep into the cave by the people who brought him there, again by elevator, and medical operations were performed on his eyes by medical robots. Both of Positive's eyes were badly damaged. After the operation, his eyes were bandaged and it was decided that the bandage would stay on for about 3 (three) months. During this time, the condition of the positive person's eyes was and would continue to be monitored with advanced biomedical devices without the bandage being untied and opened. At this stage, the affirmative continued to see, not by using his eyes, but by using a device mounted on his skull and sending signals from there to the part of the brain where the signals from the eyes are sent. There was no (consequential) loss of vision. But it was positive, and the medical robots that were trying to heal him again wanted to restore his natural vision. That is, after his eyes had healed, he would see with his eyes again, and then the electronic equipment that enabled him to see externally would be removed from his skull. Before the three months were up, a very high percentage of the positive's eyes were healthy again. There was no longer any need to keep the bandage and it was removed. In order to adapt the eyes, which had been closed for a long time, to light, a special wavelength of light was used in a special environment. In this process, that is, in this special environment, the positive person stayed for 2 (two) days and then left. He was even taken out of the cave afterwards. In order for his eyes to interact with the natural starlight. It was decided that he would stay outside, on the black surface of the planet, for at least 6 (six) months. In the meantime, from time to time, he would go down into the depths of the cave and communicate with both his parents and the parents of his dead friend, the negative. The parents of the positive had the following request from the positive: build a new spaceship to come to us and name it after your friend who burned to death. So the name of the new spaceship you're going to build is "negative". Positive had already thought about this situation before. When his parents made the same request, he got everything ready to realize it and after his stay on the surface with the robots in the depths of the cave was completed, he would start working together. After being outside for about 6 (six) months, he went back down to the depths of the cave to build a new spaceship and started to work in a more tiring, harder work tempo. The more he thought of his friend, the tighter and more serious he took his work. Because he wanted the spaceship he would name after his friend to be very modern, very advanced, in other words, to have very high-level features. Therefore, the work he did and would do was progressing in accordance with this purpose. However, this work would not last as long as the first work they did together with their friend and robots. Because there were already planning and production units. He was mostly doing revision work to make them more advanced and advanced. This seemed to take about 2-3 years. As the work continued, both his parents and the parents of the negative were watching the work in progress. Both (both) parents were satisfied with the work. Finally, a period of 2.5 years was completed and the new spaceship was ready. Then the ship was named "Negative". This name was written on the upper surface of the spaceship with the letters of a special alphabet they used, using a laser beam. The ship was about 9-10 times the volume of the first ship they built. Therefore, the word "negative" was written in the same proportion, both in capital letters and on a large scale. After the spaceship named "negative" was ready, Positive was planning to go to the grave of "positive" on his first trip. It took off towards that planet with 5 (five) robots on board. This time the spaceship would arrive in a much shorter time than the normal transportation time of 2 (two) months. The engines of the spaceship named Negative had more advanced technology than the first spaceship built. It was almost two (2) times faster. In this case, the spaceship named Negative would reach the target planet in about 1 (one) month. Although Positive continued to feel sorry for his dead friend Negative, it was not the same as before. The deadline was met and the negative spaceship landed at the landing base on the target planet. Then the positive and the 5 (five) robots with him started walking towards the area where the negative's grave was located. Since he had informed his parents before coming here, they were also on their way to the cemetery. Both the parents of the positive and the parents of the negative walked to the cemetery within 45 (forty-five) minutes. Long prayers were said and then many red and white roses were placed on the grave. The negative's mother scattered the white rose seeds she had brought with her on the grave and then poured some water. Then they sadly walked away from the cemetery. In the meantime, before leaving the cemetery, the Positive had left the masathennis racket and ball, one of the Negative's favorite things, which he had brought from the planet he had come from. After kissing his parents' hands and saying goodbye to see them again, the negative boarded the spaceship with 5 (five) robots and then the spaceship took off. He started to travel towards the planet he came from. Again, after a travel time of about 1 (one) month, they reached their planet. The door of the spaceship opened and five (5) robots got out positively and started to travel deeper into the cave with the elevator in question. Meanwhile, there was a development they were not aware of. As the spaceship was coming, a wild animal somehow got on the spaceship and then fell asleep inside the spaceship. After the ship landed, it continued to sleep for another 5-6 hours. When it woke up, it looked around, looking for a place to get out, and it came out comfortably through the still open door of the spaceship. The wild animal looked more like a snow leopard. On its new home planet, its weight and volume increased because of the differences from its old home planet. It increased in weight and volume by about 1000 (times) times. It was now bigger than the giants in the fairy tales once told on Earth. Its claws and the nails on the tips of its claws have also grown larger and sharper. The wild animal wandered randomly around the planet and stumbled into the cave where the positive and the robots were deep inside. As it wandered here and there inside the cave, it came to the elevator. The elevator door opened by itself, but the wild animal was much, much bigger than it could fit in the elevator. So it stuck one foot through the elevator door and then gave it a hard claw strike. At this moment the rope to which the elevator was attached broke and the elevator started to fall down with a great noise. Then it hit the ground hard with a great noise. Thus, the main elevator, which provided the connection of those in the depths of the cave with the outside, was disabled. However, there were 2 (two) more elevators in reserve. Until the main elevator was repaired, those 2 (two) spare elevators would be used for ascending and descending. The large number of robots going up in one of the spare elevators were confronted by the giant wild animal still in the cave. The animal was frightened by the sound and light emitted by the robots, so it ran out of the cave and disappeared from sight. A drone was also in the air to follow the animal. The live footage of the drone following the animal was being watched on a screen in the depths of the cave. Both the positive and the robots were surprised by the image. Because they had never seen an animal of this magnitude on their planet before. "I wonder where it came from?" they thought. The chase continued for hours and finally the wild animal got tired of running away. It was completely exhausted. His steps became slower and slower and he sat down as if he had fallen down. The place where he was sitting was almost a desert. Because of this, a cloud of dust covered the ground. The dust that rose from the ground and spread around had a negative effect on the animal. He was having difficulty breathing because of the dust. In the same way, those who followed him faced similar problems. The sensors on the robots were unable to communicate normally with their surroundings due to the dust covering them. Therefore, they had difficulty even detecting their own components, let alone seeing the wild animal they were following. In this way, both the robots and the animal waited for about half an hour. As the dust cloud gradually dissipated, in another sense, the surroundings were illuminated. But the wild animal had neither the strength nor the power to move even a millimeter, let alone run away again. Even after the dust cloud had completely dissipated, the robots could clearly see the animal on the ground. They threw the metal net they had brought with them on the animal and fixed it by hammering the ends of the metal to the ground with metals. Moreover, the metal net had trapped the animal almost glued to the ground. Then the robots started to build an animal prison there. After a few days, the animal came to its senses and realized the situation it was in. It used its hands, feet and torso to escape, but the result was the same. From time to time, the animal was given water and some food so that it would not die of hunger and thirst. The construction of the outdoor prison took about 4 (four) days of continuous work. A cage with iron bars was built, about 10 (ten) times the size of the animal. The bars of the cage were thick and very, very strong. The next step was to find out where the animal came from. For this, equipment was used to read the thoughts and memories of the creatures brought from the cave. But no precise and clear information could be obtained. So the animal would remain a mystery to them, except for its appearance. And so it was. Some of the robots thought "let's kill the animal", which the affirmative opposed. However, at the request of the positive, work was started to use the animal for their work. The animal would first be domesticated, and then, when this was certain, it would be released completely. However, this work seemed to take quite a long time. Because the animal, still in the cage, was almost tearing its body apart to get out. With the impact of the violent impact, its arms and legs were torn in places and blood began to ooze from them. Moreover, the blood loss was increasing. An injection was immediately given to knock the animal unconscious. The wild animal immediately fainted due to the effect of the medicine it had received with the injection. Then, when it was decided that the animal was now harmless, the top of the metal cage was opened. The animal was removed with a crane-like vehicle and transported to the cave. The medical robots first stopped the animal's bleeding. However, they were determined to keep him unconscious for a long time. After a while, the bleeding stopped completely, and then they mounted an integrated circuit inside the skull that allowed them to control every movement and behavior of the animal. In this way, the animal would behave as if it were a radio frequency-controlled circuit. So they could make the wild animal do anything they wanted. Again, after about six (6) days, the animal was fully awakened. If the animal somehow felt the electronic circuit inside its skull and wanted to remove it, the integrated circuit that sensed this would prevent the animal from doing so. It would do this by sending signals to the animal's arms, hands and fingers. The integrated circuit installed inside the skull was a multifunctional and multipurpose electronic circuit. It was even controlled in this sense, preventing the animal from removing the integrated circuit, let alone touching it. The positive had something different in mind for the wild animal. That was to turn the animal into a "spaceship". If he succeeded, the engine of the spaceship would be the animal's brain. And in order to prevent the animal from rejecting this transformation, he would use the integration built into the skull. Everything down to the smallest component and building block of the animal would be transformed into a spaceship and a building block. To do this, the robotic medical team would wait for the animal to make a full recovery and then proceed. Since the animal was very, very strong, he thought that after the positive transformation, any weapon mounted on the animal (spaceship) could be made stronger by the animal. Two weeks later, the wild animal recovered by a very large percentage and then the process of transforming it into a spaceship was started by the positive and the robots. The transformation would be from the inside of the animal to the outside. The equipment previously used for this purpose in the depths of the cave was moved by elevators to an area near the entrance of the cave (from the inside) and assembled and prepared with great precision and care. Since the animal was too big and would not fit in the elevator, it was not possible to take it deeper into the cave. Therefore, the equipment to be used in the exchange was taken upstairs. Just in case, the animal was knocked out again within a certain percentage. But this fainting was not done in such a way that the animal was 100% conscious. It was only slightly, to a certain extent, conscious. The transformation process began. The change from the center of gravity inside the animal to the outside began. The animal did not react in any way. Also, while the process was being carried out, it positively changed the brain structure of the animal to include the mathematical model that explains the operation of its own brain in every sense. This change was first made in the form of a change in the living brain, and then the animal's brain was transformed into a spaceship engine in a 100 percent sense. At the same time as the internal transformation began, the brain was being transformed into a spaceship engine. The transformation took about 7 (seven) days, with very short downtime. Thus, a brand new and very powerful spaceship was obtained in every sense. Dark blue was chosen as the color of the spaceship. Afterwards, Positive and the robots were discussing among themselves, "Can we, for any reason, transform this spaceship back into its original structure, that is, back into an animal?" Positive said "I don't think we can" and the robots around him said "no, we can't, we can't turn it back to its original form as a living being". It was time to mount weapons on the spaceship. Mostly laser weapons and some weapons that emit very powerful electromagnetic waves were mounted on the spaceship. The weapons would be controlled by the engine, which also ran the spaceship. But there was also a positive control. If for any reason the engine could not control the weapons, then the positive would take over. Now it was time to control the spaceship and its weapons. For this, an environment like a real war environment would be created and the spaceship would be tested in every sense. Since the weapons were very powerful, they chose a planet far, far away from their planet as the battle environment. Both the transformed spaceship and their own spaceship set off for this place. The journey was going to be long because the planet to be tested was very, very far away. It was estimated that the planet could be reached in four (4) months. The outbound journey had started, and after that time it was reached. And then the testing was started immediately. To check the durability of the spaceship, the ship was brought close to a star in that star system, within a certain distance. Even at very high temperatures, the spaceship was not adversely affected. In the next stage, meteorites randomly circulating in the part of the universe where they are located were directed to hit the spacecraft at high speeds (by increasing their velocity). At this stage, the asteroids hit the outer surface of the spacecraft at very different points, one after the other. Some asteroids were accelerated up to tens of times to check their durability. Aside from the negative impact on the spacecraft, the impacting meteorites would crumble. In other words, they shattered and disintegrated. So the new spaceship passed another test with flying colors. There were further endurance tests, and then the tests to see the effectiveness of the spacecraft's weapons began. Laser guns were fired at asteroids that were constantly passing by the spaceship. Just as they disintegrated on impact, when they were hit by the laser weapons, they not only disintegrated, they turned to dust, then vaporized and scattered across the universe. Next was the testing of weapons that emitted electromagnetic waves. For this, there was nothing in the area where they were located to test them and to check and measure their effectiveness. Since there were no such objects, they were going to use their own hardware in this test. These objects, the electromechanical hardware, were much, much more powerful transmitters than even GigaWatts. The spacecraft's weapons in this sense focused the electromagnetic waves they sent out on this hardware and in a short time the hardware was disabled. Thus, another weapon test was successfully concluded and completed. There were many other weapons of a different nature and design. They were tested with very different applications and all of them were successful. Thus, there were no more weapons left to test. Another test was next. That was to maximize the speed of the spaceship and to measure the endurance of the engines by moving at maximum speed for very long periods of time. To do this, the spaceship left its current location and was taken to an area where there were fewer meteorites than in the old area where the speed test was to be carried out. Once there, the spacecraft's speed was gradually increased linearly. With the engines running at maximum power, the spacecraft's speed was maximized. The spacecraft traveled at this speed for days without interruption and without interruption, and nothing negative was observed. Thus, the speed test was concluded successfully. There were some minor tests left. They were carried out after a certain period of time and all the necessary tests were completed. Then the spaceship returned to their home planet with the other spaceship and other equipment. Now they had a very powerful spaceship. They didn't know whether they could use it in a war. Because up to that moment there had been no attack or war against their planet. But what will the future show or what will happen next? Since they didn't know the answer to this question, the spaceship would protect them at a very high level, both in terms of defense and attack. In the meantime, from time to time, Positive would go to the planet where his parents were and continue to visit them. Positive told the robots, "There is no other living being here except me. That is why I am often bored. You exist, but each of you is nothing more than electromechanical hardware." He said to the robots, "Let's go out in our new spaceship and look for a planet with intelligent, thinking beings. And if we find one, let's bring one of them here, okay?" Affirmative: "No, that won't work, we don't know if the creature will want to come here and we don't know how it will behave and act when it gets here. That is why it is not possible. Even though I am the only living being on this planet and I am bored, there is nothing else to do." So life on their planet began to resume naturally again. The positive, who was in video communication with his parents from time to time, was told that his father was sick. "Don't they have medical robots there to cure it?" asked the positive. His father said: "They do, but it is temporary and not permanent. The natural conditions of the planet we are on made me sick. The robots' advice was to go to another suitable planet". Positive: "so dad, what kind of planet will this be?" His father: "the gravity should be less than 1/2 of the current planet and it should rain a lot, so they said." Positive: "Dad, well, me and the robots with me will set off right away to find a planet like you said." Father: "OK". After the preparations were completed in a short time, the journey began with the new spaceship to find the planet with the mentioned characteristics. The spaceship traveled outside the star system they were in. They discovered many planets in terms of gravitational force, but in none of them did it rain, not constantly, not at all. Five (5) months had passed since they started their journey, but they still had not come across the planet they wanted to find. Two days later, they came across a planet where it rained continuously. But it was not raining "water" but "acid". And on some of them, large and small stones were falling all the time. After another two months, they found a planet where it was raining. However, the rainfall here was not continuous but periodic. They continued to wander for a few more months, but finally settled on that planet. The distance of the planet they discovered was about 2 (two) months from the planet where their parents were staying. On the planet they found, they built a single-story, multi-room horizontal house for the parents they would bring here. There were other works. In a total of 3 (three) months they accomplished most of what was necessary. Then they went to their planet to pick up their parents with a spaceship transformed from an animal. Taking the parents of the negative, they set off for the planet they had discovered with 5 (five) people and many robots. During the journey, the father of the positive got a little worse. Finally they reached the planet. By coincidence, when they stepped out of the spaceship, they found themselves in a very heavy rain. The rain was healing his father both physically and spiritually. Here the water drops of the rain did not have to touch his father. Feeling the presence of the rain and experiencing it was a very effective medicine for his treatment. After about three hours the rain stopped and the influence of the star in the star system in which the planet was located began to take effect on the planet. So the weather started to warm up. When they arrived on the planet, it was just coming out of winter. In other words, a spring with plenty of rain was waiting for them. (At least that's what they guessed.) They immediately went to the house that had been prepared by the positive and robots. The house had a total of 10 (ten) rooms, 3 (three) halls, 4 (four) toilets, 2 (two) bathrooms, a library, a gym, a cinema, a theater, a health room, a laboratory, etc. There was also a long elliptical walkway around the house. Then they decided to build a shelter, "just in case". They were not going to build it under the ground. Because that would not be suitable for the father of the positive. They would build it outside, but with the highest level of camouflage. In other words, it would in no way be separate or different from the natural structure of the planet. When someone who did not know would look at it, they would not recognize it as a "shelter", they would perceive it as a part of the natural structure of the planet. Two (2) days after their arrival on the planet, they started to build the shelter in question. However, the construction of the shelter was going to take much longer than the construction of their house. Because in addition to the construction, there was also camouflage. Seven (7) months had passed since their arrival on the planet. They wanted to make an "expedition" to see "what's on the planet". They started the expedition with five people and robots. The first thing they noticed was that the planet seemed to have no plains or flat areas. There were many hills, mountains and forests. As they traveled uphill, the others, except for the positive and the robots, were getting quite tired. A few hundred meters from the top of a hill, they heard some sounds. When they walked towards where the sound was coming from, they saw many houses made of tree stumps and in each of them they saw many small children. They estimated the ages of the children to be between 4/5 and 11/12. Seeing people and robots they had never seen before, the children ran from side to side in the houses they were in and ran away, screaming at the same time. Seeing that the children were scared, they moved away from them and stood in a corner of the house. Thus, they spent about half an hour in mutual silence. Then they gave the children the hazelnut chocolates they had brought with them. Of course, they did not have enough for all the children. They gave them to as many children as there were chocolates. Some of the children ate the chocolates while others took them and threw them against the wall of the house. Then they talked among themselves and picked up the chocolates they had thrown and started eating them. Most of the children came to 5 (five) people and the robots and asked them in their own language if they had "another chocolate". Positive and his companions did not understand the language spoken by the children, but they understood that they wanted chocolate from their hand gestures. On the other hand, as far as they could see, they were trying to understand why "hundreds of children" were left here alone. They saw a computer in a corner of the room. Positive immediately went and turned it on. As soon as the computer was turned on, a video played. The answer to the question they had just been looking for was in this video. The video lasted about 2 (two) hours. They all watched it until the end. When it was over, they realized that they had been brought here to protect children from a "deadly disease" that had developed on a planet. They realized that the parents of the children had died because of that deadly disease. So they realized that they had made a positive decision, a positive decision to choose this planet and to bring their parents here. Because the parents of the children had also been brought to this planet so that their children could continue to live. They took the oldest child, as far as they could guess, and went to the children in the other houses. The boy, probably twelve (12) years old, talked to the other children and told them "not to be afraid of these unexpected intruders". So they went in and out of dozens of houses containing hundreds of children. They estimated that there were around 10,000 (ten thousand) children. They also realized that not much time had passed since the children had been brought here. The food for the children would only last for a limited period of time. For this reason, the robots that arrived with the positive immediately started to set up facilities to produce food products. From bread bakeries, to fish canneries, to chocolate production facilities and more. However, the number of robots arriving on the planet and the equipment they brought were insufficient. For this, another spaceship brought a large number of robots and materials. There were 2 (two) spaceships in total. No harm was supposed to come to them. However, in the future, just in case, they decided that they needed to increase the number of spaceships much, much more than 2 (two). In this sense, work was initiated for this purpose both on their own planet and on the planet they had come from. In the meantime, five (5) people and robots started to think about how and what kind of education would be given to children and what professions they should have when they grow up in the future. There were 10,000 (ten thousand) children in total. They decided to distribute them equally for each profession. Engineers, doctors, soldiers, technicians and technicians, athletes, musicians, lawyers, judges, nurses, writers, accountants, waiters, waitresses, cleaners, carpenters, painters and so on. Education and training was to begin for those under the age of 8 (eight) when they reached that age. For those who were older, it would start immediately. Three (3) years had passed since they arrived on this new planet. Fifteen (15) spaceships arrived and landed on the planet, one after the other, unexpectedly. Out of them came a large number of teams of people, mostly middle-aged and elderly people - parents and other relatives who had brought and left their children here to protect them from the deadly epidemic. - Immediately arriving in the area where the spaceships had landed, he positively asked them "who they were, where they had come from and for what purpose". "We have managed to control the deadly epidemic on our planet and we have completely stopped and eradicated it, now it is time to take our children back to our planet" was the reply. Positive also gave information about himself and said that the education and training of the children had begun. The parents of the children said, "Let's ask the children one by one, let those who want to stay here stay, and let's take those who don't want to go back to our planet." Positive agreed and they started asking the children one by one. About 75%, or 7,500 children, said they wanted to stay here and continue, and the remaining 2,500 children said they wanted to go back to their planet. Those who wanted to go back were taken on spaceships and the ships departed. The parents and other relatives of the children who stayed here decided to check on their children at very frequent intervals. The children accepted this idea. Thus, education and training, which had been interrupted for a short time, resumed. The children were especially eager to learn mathematics and math subjects that were not available today (2000s). Among those topics were: the creation of multivariable functions that express the increase and decrease of dimension when traveling to universes of different dimensions, finding formulas that explain existence and non-existence and the transformation between them when nothing existed (i.e. before creation) except God/Allah. Even though some of the topics that explain the content of the course are the subject of physics, they were basically tried to be solved from a mathematical point of view. In these years, it was even possible to say that physics was a sub-branch of mathematics. Apart from the known theories, the aim was to develop formulas to express the communication between living and non-living matter in the process starting from the formation of all universes up to that moment, not in the sense of social sciences but in the sense of science. Studies on "how we can prevent" the situation of going forward or backward in time depending on the speed of travel, which has been the subject of "modern physics" in the past years. For this purpose, the emphasis was often on changing the structure of the vehicle in which one was traveling and building it with different components. In addition, there were many other topics... Some of the children had a request that was more than positive. And that was: "can you make us resistant to epidemics and deadly diseases?" This was both a request from the children and a request from their parents. Positive and robots did not have any previous work on this subject. Therefore, rather than responding in this sense, the answer was given as follows: "there must be planets that have no risk of any disease, no matter what's on them, and that they don't get sick. If we can discover such planets, we will be able to respond to your purpose with a different solution". In addition, some of the children had very different requests: "Can you give us the training of the commandos in the Army of the Republic of Turkey on Earth, which does not exist in the videos we were shown before, so can you train us like them?" Positive: "It would definitely not be right to say that we can do this in a hundred percent sense. But we can ensure that you have the characteristics of commandos in today's conditions. But not at this age. We can do it in at least 9/10 years." Children: "Well, can't you start a study now to start or prepare for those years?" Positive: "that would be fine, we can start as you say." On the other hand, the new spaceship (transformed from a wild animal) left the planet and set out to find a planet "free of disease". The ship was equipped with a wide range of equipment, tools and instruments to make a wide range of different measurements on almost every subject. For this purpose, they would make measurements on the planets they came across and found suitable, and try to find the most suitable one. This time there were no living beings on board. The ship was filled with electromechanical robots. They had limited the travel time for this purpose. Because they had only two (2) spaceships. They did not want to use the many spaceships that brought the parents of the children for their own purposes because they did not know them very well. They limited this period to a maximum of 5 (five) months. In other words, the new spaceship had to return after 5 (five) months at the latest. Also, since the time was limited, the spaceship was to travel at speeds close to maximum speed in order to study as many different planets as possible. Positive and the robots decided so. They had great confidence in the new ship in terms of durability and strength. However, they were faced with an unexpected situation. When the spaceship entered the legal boundaries of a planet, it was immediately subjected to a laser beam attack and the ship shattered in its position. So the ship was destroyed. Positive and the robots were muttering amongst themselves "what did we expect?". So they were left with only 1 (one) spaceship. They immediately went back to the planet where that cave was located and started building spaceships in large numbers, but not too large in volume. They were working very hard. They wanted to build as many spaceships as possible, day and night. They also moved the production lines inside and outside the cave, instead of keeping them only in the depths of the cave. Within weeks, the production of spaceships began in series. All of these spaceships had one distinctive feature: "it was not the weapons systems they could carry, but their speed, which was very, very high." Thus, if they were faced with a situation like the one with the destroyed spaceship, they would immediately accelerate to high speeds to escape the attack. For this purpose, the spaceships in mass production are small and very, very light. In the first phase, 25 (twenty-five) spaceships were produced. The reason why they were so few in number was that they had very different characteristics. When they traveled at the speed of light they did not turn into energy, when they passed the speed of light they did not go backwards in time, when they traveled at speeds up to the speed of light they did not go forward in time, and their length did not change in any way depending on the speed of travel, but remained constant. This was not something that had been realized until that moment. The space ships they produced were given these properties by the elements they used to make them. Because there were elements with very different atomic structures on the planet they were on, and they built their spaceships using them. The atoms of the elements contained a wide range of what we would now call today's "artificial intelligence" components. For example, when the speed of light was exceeded, they realized not to become energy and not to go back in time by saying: "at this very moment, the atom reconfigures itself so that while the outer surface of the spaceship is traveling above the speed of light, the inner part of the spaceship is under control to prevent any changes from occurring on this surface." This was due to the fact that God/Allah had created very different elements in different universes, in different celestial bodies (stars, planets, asteroids, etc...). There may be elements containing atoms with these properties in the universe in which we (Earth) now exist, but we do not have the knowledge of this (i.e. whether it exists or not). This implies the following: "to build spaceships that can travel at much higher speeds and discover more different celestial bodies in our universe." By the way, positively, because he loved children so much, he was thinking of building a spaceship for each of them. The number of children left on the planet was 7,500. Therefore, the goal of Positive and the robots was to build at least 7,500 spaceships in the shortest possible time. The only thing they had trouble doing was shaping the metals composed of those elements mentioned earlier. (In other words, processing them.) Here, the shaping process was not done by heating the metal, by increasing its temperature. They used a direct laser beam for this purpose. But the problem was that it was very, very difficult for them to obtain a continuous, uninterrupted laser beam. At this stage, they transformed their work into another stage in order to obtain the laser beam. On the planet they were on, there were many substances that spontaneously emitted light in line with their natural properties. In the first stage, the positive and robots thought of strengthening the light emitted by these natural light sources and converting it into laser beams with additional work. In this sense, they sought to build hardware like the amplifiers used in today's electronic circuits that increase the power of signals. They did not favor the idea of increasing the power of light with optical components. They focused on different solutions. They thought of combining the elements in question with the sources of light-emitting substances, that is, integrating them. Their idea was successful. The different components of the atoms of the elements increased the power of the light emitted from the light source in direct proportion to the amount of elements added to it. After many stages of testing, they decided to collect the naturally luminescent substances in one part of the planet. This process did not take long and was completed in a matter of days. Then, with the addition of the elements, everything was ready for them to use the light, which had increased in power, to process the metals they used to build spaceships in the way they wanted. Seven thousand spaceships began to be built, each one for one child. This was a minimum, and more would be built. In a relatively short period of time, about 2 (two) years, 7,000 spaceships were produced. While production was going on, the 7,000 children who remained on the planet were trained to operate the spaceships. Since the ships were small and generally had few functions, each child was trained to become a professional in terms of the ship they would use. After the production was completed, all of the children boarded their own spaceships and took off in groups of a certain number, leaving the planet they were on and traveling around the universe they were in. At the front of the seven thousand ships, they were guarded by a spaceship with high combat capabilities, which was assigned to protect them "just in case". The others were in groups of 50 (fifty), one after the other, moving through the void of the universe. The children's journey in their spaceship was not a long journey of exploration, but rather a short journey of controlling the ship, testing it and seeing what it was all about. After about two days, all the ships returned to the planet. Then normal education and training resumed. After a long time, the parents of the 7,000 children who remained on the planet came back to the planet in spaceships. They wanted to convince their remaining children to return to their planet. In fact, each mother and father spent days in dialog with their children, insisting that they return. But none of the children wanted to go back and said they were "very happy" where they were. They added that "now each of us has a spaceship, and this spaceship is not a toy, but a real spaceship". In the face of their children's determined and confident attitude, their parents gave up their desire to "take them back" and then asked, "If you don't want to come back, then we will come to see you periodically, okay?" The children chorused in unison and said, "Of course, yes". Thus, their parents left the same planet for the third time. In the meantime, the parents of the Negative, who had died earlier, had fallen ill in their longing for the Negative, and both of them had died of illnesses caused by grief. Thus, apart from the affirmative and his parents, there were no living beings left from their former planet. In this way, with various practices, another 10 (ten) years came and went. The parents of the negative were also old. Both of them no longer traveled alone on their planet, but with a companion robot. In the meantime, the positive thought of organizing competitions and giving prizes to the children to make them more successful in many areas. For example; "to pass through and exit the regions where there are many asteroids in the shortest time without hitting them with the spaceship, to find different celestial bodies that are beyond the ones known so far, to be able to go without eating or drinking for the longest time while traveling with the spaceship (especially applied to those who received commando training) ..." These were competitions with prizes that the children could and would do individually, that is, individually. There were also competitions to be organized by the teams (groups) that the children would come together as many times as they wanted among themselves. For this number, a lower and upper limit was determined positively and by robots. This was the formation of teams (groups) with a minimum of 5 (five) people and a maximum of 15 (fifteen) people. In addition, there was no distinction between boys and girls when forming groups. The competitions to be held in groups would include (some of) the following: Best hiding, best leaving no trace, best tracking, best offense, best defense, highest average speed, best exploration, best coordination, best management, etc. It was decided to organize a competition with the joint decision of the positive and robots. There would be 10 (ten) teams (groups) in the competition. One group, which was decided which one it would be, would escape from the other 9 (nine) groups. In other words, they would try to lose track of them. If the time to cover their tracks was achieved in 4 (four) days without interruption, the escaping group would win the competition and receive the big prize. However, if the opposite happens, that is, if 9 (nine) groups do not lose sight of the fleeing group, then these 9 (nine) groups will win the competition and the big prize will be distributed equally among the groups. The question here was not whether or not to lose/ not to lose sight of or to lose/not to lose sight of, but in the sense of not being able to catch them with the radars on spaceships. For this purpose, both the group that would escape and the group that would follow were given kits that could fit inside the spaceships consisting of a large number of electronic circuit elements and electronic hardware (components) so that they could use them during the competition and design electronic circuits. Since there was at least one engineer in each group, they had to design and make usable circuits for disappearing/not disappearing with the circuits that the engineer in question would make using his/her knowledge of electronics. The engineers were computer, electronics, electrical, mechatronics, control and automation, etc. The preparations were completed in 1 (one) day and 10 (ten) teams (groups) left the planet with their spaceships to start the competition. The number of people in the groups, and therefore the number of spaceships, was the same, but there were cases where it was not the same. For example, one group could have five spaceships while another group could have 7,8...,15. The team (group) to escape had exactly 10 (ten) people/spaceship. The competition started on the day and at the time previously determined by the event organizers. All groups started the competition on the same line. In other words, there was no logic that the group that would escape or lose track of the other groups would be in the front and the other groups would be in the back. The group that escaped first did not accelerate to high speeds, they preferred a linear speed increase and increased their speed over time. However, since the nine (9) groups following them followed the same logic, there was no such thing as losing the trail. All the spaceships in the fleeing group had electronic circuits of very different design in order to evade the radar of the pursuing spaceships. There was 1 (one) person on each spaceship. The ships were put into "auto-motion" mode and only one person on board was making electronic circuits. They could also control the spaceship with their "thoughts". This situation was made possible by the use of a highly advanced scientific technology in terms of control and management of these ships. Each ship was equipped with electronic equipment that recorded every moment. One (1) week had passed since the start of the competition and the trail of the fleeing group was found on all the other ships in pursuit. The pursuing ships had both active radars and passive radars. The aim of the engineers in the fleeing group was to render both types of radar inoperable, that is, to disable them. To do this, they needed to build very powerful transmitters, but the electronic kits they were given did not have these features. Therefore, they opted for the following: they combined the gravitational forces of each celestial body they passed on a line and focused them on the radars of the spacecraft in pursuit. They set this time period to be 5 (five) days. Thus, they completed the 4 (four) days set to win the competition by losing their tracks. When the positive and robots, who had been watching and following everything that was happening since the beginning of the competition, saw the situation, they informed the "groups" that the competition was over. Thus, the group that escaped completed the competition by winning. More electronic equipment was given as gifts. However, some of the winning group also asked for the chocolates with hazelnuts and pistachios that were given to them as children. So a large number of these chocolates were also given to the winning group/team. After a period of about 2 (two) weeks, the positive and the robots decided to have another competition. This time 10 (ten) groups would compete. The subject of the competition was: "which group would be able to get out of a region of the universe far, far away from their planet, where meteorites are densely populated and in motion, the sooner (without any damage / without the meteorites hitting the spaceships)." This time would be calculated by averaging the transit times of all the spaceships in that group. Whichever group/team had the smallest transit time would win the competition. Ten (10) groups were randomly selected from more than ten (10) groups who volunteered to participate in the competition and traveled to the region in question with their spaceships to compete. Unlike the previous competition, these groups had an equal number of people/spaceships. This was decided positively. There were 7 (seven) people/spaceships in each group/team. Again, after all spaceships were positioned so that they were on the same line, the competition started with the affirmative giving the start command. The spaceships were trying to pass the area in question as soon as possible by experiencing a very intense non-collision situation. Some of the ships used by 4 (four) of the ten groups were colliding violently with meteorites. In fact, due to the impact of this collision, the spaceships were thrown even further back from their starting positions. Some of the spaceships were even completely disabled. It had been about 3 (three) weeks since the competition had started and no group had yet crossed the area in question. After a few more days, the number of groups that had crossed that area without any damage to their spaceships was 3 (three). The winner of the competition would be one of these 3 (three) groups/teams. The crossing times were calculated with the electronic equipment on board the ships and the group with the smallest average crossing time was the 9th (ninth) group/team. The people on the damaged ships returned to their planets in the ships they had used without experiencing any negativity in this sense. Those whose ships were damaged beyond control were taken to the planet with additional "towing ships". The average transit time of the 9th (ninth) winning group was 3 (three) weeks + 5 (five) hours. This was the smallest of the 3 (three) groups that completed the competition. On their way back to their planets, they followed an elliptical trajectory further away from the region where they competed. The gifts were both positive and thought out and prepared by the robots even before the competition started. Those whose ships were damaged would be repaired and maintained. Since there were many research and development laboratories on the planet, scientific technology development was at an advanced level. Those members of the winning group who had previously wanted to work in these laboratories but could not, were given the right to work in these laboratories. There were seven people, 5 (five) of them wanted to work in these laboratories, while the remaining 2 (two) people told Positive and Robots that they were very worn out and tired and that they wanted to take a vacation to take a break from their education for a while. Positive and robots accepted this request of 2 (two) people. Apart from the logic of going to the sea or going to a forest area as a vacation, there was a much different approach. What they thought of as a vacation and what they wanted to do was this: "go to the biggest library on the planet, buy any book they want for one (1) month and read it as long as they want. - No more than one month. - "- As you can see, study, that is, learning, developing science and technology, researching and creating new inventions and discoveries, was in the blood of the people who were brought to this planet when they were small children. This was their purpose and philosophy of life. After two (2) competitions, the positive and the robots decided to have a third competition. After this third competition, the competitions would take a break for a while. The subject or content of this competition was as follows: equal numbers of spaceships in each group, to determine the group that had the least contact with weapons sent from other ships. Therefore, the group with the least contact (after taking the average contact values) would be declared the winner of the competition. The weapons in question here were not real weapons as we know them. If they had been, the weapon could have made contact with another spaceship and partially or completely damaged it. Instead, special wavelengths of light sent from linear light emitting sources from one ship to another would be detected by the sensors on the target ship upon contact, and the current contact value would be increased by one with each contact. Then the average contact values of the groups would be taken and the winner of the competition would be determined. If there were any ships/ships that were not exposed to any contact during the competition, they would be given special prizes. 10 (ten) groups/teams would participate in the competition. Each group had the same number of people/spaceships and their number was 10 (ten). After the arrival of the spaceships to the area where the competition was to take place, the competition started, as in previous competitions, with the command of the affirmative. In groups, the ships both chased each other and avoided each other to avoid contact. There was also a special rule for this competition only. If ships in the same group came into weapons contact with each other, both the contacting and the contacted ships would be withdrawn from the competition. For this reason, there was no electronic equipment on the ships to determine or indicate whether they were in the same group or not. The ships of each group were painted in a different color. The sailors were to use their naked eyes and, if necessary, optical devices (binoculars, etc.) to find the ships that were not from their own group and try to bring their weapons into contact with them. The competition had been going on for 3 (three) days and no spaceship had not been contacted. This meant that there was no ship to receive the special prize. The competition continued for four more days and after the completion of one week, at the request of the affirmative, the competition was completed. Since the numbers and therefore averages were calculated at the exact moment of contact, the winning group/team was immediately announced at the end of the competition. The winning group was group 2 (two) and the average contact value was 15.XXX. All the ships then returned to their planets. The prizes were immediately distributed to the members of the group related to the ships' arrival on the planet. Thus, a total of

3 (three) competitions were left behind until that moment. Positive and the robot team that was always with him intended to hold more competitions. However, not at that moment but after a certain period of time. While the natural flow continued on the planet, unexpectedly and unpredictably, a spaceship of gigantic dimensions began to approach their planet. After a short time, it passed through the planet's atmosphere and landed in a suitable place. Positive and many robots, who had been following the situation from the beginning, arrived at the place where the alien spaceship was to land. A part of the spaceship, which from the outside was not clear whether it was a door or not, opened. Then five (5) armed soldiers came out, then an unarmed one. After that, another 5 (five) armed soldiers came out again. After the eleven people exited the spaceship, they started walking towards the location of the positive, with the unarmed one in the lead. There was a distance of about 30-35 meters between them. When the one in front and the positive came face to face, the positive said: "Who are you people and why did you come to our planet unannounced and for what purpose?" The other asked: "I should ask this question to you. You probably confuse the boundaries of your planet with the boundaries of the universe you are in. Many spaceships that took off from your planet without our permission were playing a game or a contest in a galaxy neighboring our planet. Did you get permission for this? Without permission, you mistook the universe as your own universe and you were running around in it with your spaceships. This time we attributed it to your ignorance and ignorance. If you do something like this again without our permission, we will destroy your ship with its contents, so don't say you didn't know, just so you know". In the face of such precise, clear, open and confident speech of the positive person in front of him: "who are you and why do we need your permission?" The other asked: "it seems that you do not have any knowledge about the management of the universe. In this universe, the planets that contain living beings take over the

61

management of the universe in every sense of the word in certain periods, that is, in rotation. Their management continues until the next ones take over. Right now it is our planet's turn to be the ruler of our universe. I am the president of our planet, therefore I am the ruler of the universe right now. I think you understand now." Positive: "I understand, but as you just said, we didn't know that the universe has periodic rulers. From now on, if we want to do something like what we have done before, we apply for permission from whoever is in charge at the time." The manager said: "ok then." Positive: "since we have agreed, let us host you and your soldiers for a while and then you can leave whenever you want." Administrator: "yes". Positive: "If I wanted to introduce you to those people you just complained about, would you accept?" Manager: "of course." Positive: "then we should all walk together for about 20/25 minutes." Manager: "can't we go by car?" Affirmative: "of course we can, but I didn't say that specifically, I thought you should see the planet where your spacecraft landed." Manager: "okay, you thought right". After a twenty minute walk, they reached the location of the groups/teams that had participated in 3 (three) different competitions. There were also the small spaceships they had used during the competition. The manager asked one of them: "how fast your spacecraft was going, and from time to time we were losing traces of you with the radars we were using. You must have been doing some work inside the ship for this purpose." Contestant: "Yes, yes. We were making electronic circuits as part of our competition. These would affect the radar and similar devices at a certain distance and prevent them from working." Administrator: "Just as I guessed, now I am more sure. So what kind of application was this? Because our radars are very powerful. How did you prevent it from working, won't you tell us the real reason?" Contestant: "according to you - unfortunately - I won't tell you, because this is our scientific and technological secret." Manager: "OK, well, let it remain your secret." Positive: "you just said that the management of the universe is given to the planets in turn..." Administrator: "yes". Positive: "then will it be our planet's turn to become a ruler?" Administrator: "yes, of course it will, but I don't know when, maybe you will be the ruler after me, or maybe it will be your turn after 500,000 years, for example, it is impossible to know or predict" Affirmative: "why?" Director: "because which planet will be ruled is beyond my knowledge and is something that the Association of the Rulers of the Universe knows. So no one outside this association knows how and on what basis they decide. But there is one thing that has been whispered about for many years. And that is that every time they choose a planet to be the ruler, this union works on different mathematical functions and they are constantly improving them. Even they don't know this, but after completing the functions each time and giving values to the variables used there, it is not clear who the ruler will be according to the result. So the Universe Managers' Union doesn't know anything until the result." Positive: "I am trying to understand." Administrator: "yes." Affirmative: "so where is this Union of Universe Rulers, I mean where do they stay?" Manager: "they don't have a fixed place, they all come from the same nation of origin. In other words, their origin is Turkish. Therefore, they have all the characteristics of Turks from their past history. So they are nomads. They go from one planet to another, maybe there is no planet in the universe that they have not set foot on, or if there is, their number is probably very, very small." Affirmative: "Do you know where they are now, or can we contact them?" Manager: "I don't know where they are or what planet they are on. It is impossible to communicate with them. Because they can communicate with whomever they want, even if others want it, if they don't want it, it is not possible to communicate. It doesn't matter whether it's live face-to-face communication or electronic communication..." Affirmative: "We are going to have some competitions later, as you mentioned, we need your permission." Manager: "Yes, that's right". Positive: "So, after you leave here, how and where can we find you and contact you before the competition and get your permission?" Manager: "Now I am going to give you an electronic device that will allow you to communicate with the Director no matter who he is and no matter what planet he is from. With it you will always be able to communicate with the Director. I will also give you an electronic circuit diagram of the hardware, just in case, so that you can do the same if the hardware we are going to give you is lost or malfunctions. Take care of both of them like your own two eyes. Otherwise, if you want to make an application without permission in the future, this may cause life-threatening dangers for you." Positive: "ok, done". Administrator: "The communication medium used by this device is a special structure and something that is not in the normal nature of the universe." Affirmative: "What is not in nature does not exist, so where do you get this and use it?" Manager: "Yes, it doesn't exist in the universe we are in now, but it is something we found and brought from another universe, and even if our universe disappears, this communication medium will continue to exist and survive because it doesn't belong to this universe." Positive: "It was brought from another universe, so it must be something quite interesting and different. But is it possible for us to see it in any way?" Manager: "Unfortunately, it is not possible. Because we can somehow see what is naturally present in our own universe. But this one, the medium of communication is very, very different, so neither you nor we can see it." Positive: "In this case, we will be able to communicate whenever we want as long as the device we are using is active." Administrator: "Yes, exactly. Now, after this information we have presented to you, we can leave your planet. It is time to leave." Affirmative: "As you wish, as you wish..." After a short conversation, the soldiers and the Director re-boarded the spaceship they had landed on and then, a few minutes later, took off from the planet. By this time the communication device in question was in the hands of the positive. He was examining it in great detail, both looking at the electronic circuit diagram and looking at the device. Although the circuit diagram was a classical circuit diagram, there were electronic circuit elements that they did not know. Their representation in the diagram was also different. Most of the elements were available to them, but there were also some that were not. When they had to reconstruct the circuit for some reason, they were thinking "where can I find the missing electronic circuit elements" when they saw a box next to their feet. The lid of the box read: "elements needed for the circuit diagram". Positively, he immediately took the box on the ground, removed the adhesive tape on it and opened the box. Inside the box was a sealed and transparent bag. Inside were many electronic circuit elements. Immediately tearing the top of the bag, Positive took the elements inside one by one, examined them and then put them back in the bag. The electronic circuit elements in question, the ones he had seen for the first time, were much more numerous than the others. With the box and the robots beside him, Positive left the area on foot. As they were walking positively, he was planning to organize another competition. As he was going back and forth in his thoughts about what the subject could be, he decided to organize an "attack competition" this time. For this, a large number of target materials would be prepared, each with a different geometric shape. Their speed would be random. So, for example, they could stop suddenly while traveling at high speed, or increase their speed hundreds of thousands of times while traveling at a slow speed. The direction and direction of movement would also change randomly. It was decided to produce at least 150,000 of these specialized hardware. Sensors would also be placed inside each one. When these items were subjected to an armed intervention, the sensors inside would detect it and send a signal to the planet that they had been "hit". As the weapons of each group and their spaceships are different, the sensors in the hardware would also be able to detect and recognize the shooter. Thus, we would know which spaceship of which group hit how many targets. Then, the total number of hardware shot by the participating groups/teams would be calculated, and naturally, the highest number would win the competition. Similar to previous competitions, 10 (ten) groups would participate in the competition and each group would have 8 (eight) spaceships/person/competitors. The preparations for the competition were completed. Now it was time to get permission from the Director. Positively, using the equipment given to him, he communicated with the Administrator and said that he "asked for permission". The Administrator accepted, that is, gave "permission". After a very short conversation lasting a few seconds, the spaceships and the target equipment left the planet for the competition. The target equipment did not leave the planet by any other means, but directly by themselves. This was preferred because there were already 150,000 of them and there was no spaceship in which they could all fit. The competition zone outside the planet has been reached. Now all that was left was for the positive to give the command "start the competition". And the contest began. The targeted equipment moved randomly while the spaceships were chasing them in order to shoot them down. The duration of the competition was limited to four (4) hours, which was much shorter than previous competitions. Four hours of chasing and shooting resulted in 123,000 hits out of 150,000 pieces of hardware. The others completed the competition without any hits. In terms of the groups participating in the competition, the group that recorded the most hits among the 10 (ten) groups was the 7th (seventh) group, and the total number of hits of this group was 78,000, which is a very high numerical value compared to the other groups. The group with the lowest number of hits was group 2 (two), and the total number of hits of this group was not even a number to be considered, but a number, and that number was 4 (four). The fact that there was such an abyssal difference between the groups participating in the competition, both the positive and the robots were quite surprised. The majority of the members of the first/winning group 7 (seven) were civil engineers and architects. This clearly showed that their engineering knowledge could be used to achieve success in different fields. The group with four hits were mostly painters and musicians. Naturally, one can make an opinion about the success of the work to be done according to the profession one has or does, but there are also values such as talent and so on. Probably the group with the least number of hits/accuracies had such a negative impact. When the winning group came to the positive and robots, they were asked "Would you like to join our armed forces?". They replied, "Although we would like there to be no war and no such negativity, this situation is a formation that started with the creation of living beings by God/Allah and will continue until the extinction of living beings (whether human or animal). Perhaps then the war will continue between robots made by living beings - the war - somehow changing its meaning and structure. We would also like to join the army, but not in the sense of using weapons, but to work on hitting the targets of the weapons from 12 (twelve) and to train the armed forces personnel in this regard. They said, "We think this would be better for us." And he said, "Okay, that's fine." Work was then done to initiate the necessary procedures. Positive also met one by one with the representatives of the group with the lowest number of hits and asked them "why were you so unsuccessful?". The answer he received from each of them one by one had one thing in common: "The night before the competition, we did not sleep until the morning and we had a headache. The total number of hits/hits, which was 4 (four), was purely coincidental, 0 (zero) would have been more logical and correct." After listening to the positive group, he asked the winning group "do you want any additional financial reward or gift?". The answer was "no, no". Then another competition was over and the ten (10) participating groups went back to their normal jobs and duties. There was also the following practice. In the competitions held so far and in the competitions to be held, the resumes of the members of the winning group were written in the sky with a laser beam, each in a different color. This writing was to continue as long as the universe they were in existed, that is, until it disappeared. The laser beam used for the writing was obtained in a very different way. The way or the method was as follows: "there was a ready source, which was the star in the star system they were in. The diffuse reflected light emitted from the star was converted into laser beams by means of transducer interfaces. This ensured that the writing would remain for the life of the star. After the end of the star's life, i.e. its destruction, dark matter and dark energy, which are found in very high percentages in almost every universe, would be used to obtain laser beams. The work of the research and development laboratories on the planet on this subject had begun long, long before. In one of the research and development laboratories on the planet, a study was being conducted. Whatever universe it is, if it contains something (living matter or non-living matter, or matter that fluctuates between the two, that is, its state is variable), the gravitational force that it possesses can be used to control that thing through waves. If it can be accomplished, let's say by using the information coming in through gravitational waves from trillions and trillions of trillions and trillions of kilometers away into a universe, to understand what is in question and then to control it in the desired way through the same line of communication (through gravitational waves). However, since there is a path that the outgoing and incoming information has to take, there is time that has to pass. For example, the control information could arrive millions of years later, and the response from it could arrive millions of years later. In this case, every work done on this subject needs to be recorded down to the finest detail. Because after those who sent the control information die, their great-grandchildren's great-grandchildren will also die in the millions of years to come. Since the same is true for the future response, the recipient of the response will look at the information that has been done and recorded up to that point in order to know which application/

problem it is the answer to. Only in this way can intergenerational work be tracked. Work was being done in another lab on how to make this time "instantaneous". If this can be achieved, the distance and time limits in terms of communication will be completely removed and everything will be instantaneous. The goal of this work was clear. In other words, to remove the borders/turn them into zero, for which a different study was being carried out. Whatever universe there is, there is a starting point. And this very moment has traces, or remnants, in the universe after the universe began to form. If these traces or remnants can be found, any kind of instantaneous or zero-time communication can be achieved through them (using them as a springboard, for example). The lab workers first tried to discover this in their own universe. They prepared a plan to go in groups to different regions of their own universe to see if there are any common features, and if so, what are they? They would look for answers to these and similar questions. If they could find them, they would use them to carry out more extensive research with other universes to see if they had anything in common with the universe they were in. If they succeeded, they would have proved both that all universes originated from the same point and that there is at least one common feature that applies to all of them. - When there was only God/Allah and no universe had yet been created, everything existed and did not exist in today's terms. In other words, both states were valid at the same time. While the beginning of universes was occurring in this region in question, the beginning of the transformation of the smallest volume in this region into the gigantic universes of today was actually occurring. This region and today's universes are not the same. Just like in the logic that there is data but it has not been transformed into information but has been transformed later. Therefore, there is no time and space limit in this region. Everything is in the same place at the same time. If we can adapt this structure to the universe we are in now, or if we can make that change, then the boundaries of time and space will disappear. All living things and inanimate matter will be everywhere and at all times. Just as the size of the universe for living beings is beyond the limits of the mind, the same universe for God/Allah is much, much smaller than a point we know. The universe(s) that began to form with the big bang may not mean anything in terms of its size in addition to its main regions, or it may be just like the logic of a region seen in a mirror. Another approach is that there may have been a universe structure completely below the original region, spreading further downwards. (Figure -1-.) - For this purpose, groups of thousands of people, with the knowledge of probability and robots, set off for different parts of the universe. Since previous spaceships were built for one person, they built spaceships large enough to accommodate a large number of people at the same time to be used in this study. The smallest of the 20 (twenty) spaceships built for this purpose was capable of holding at least 2,000 people. The largest one had a capacity of 25,000 people.

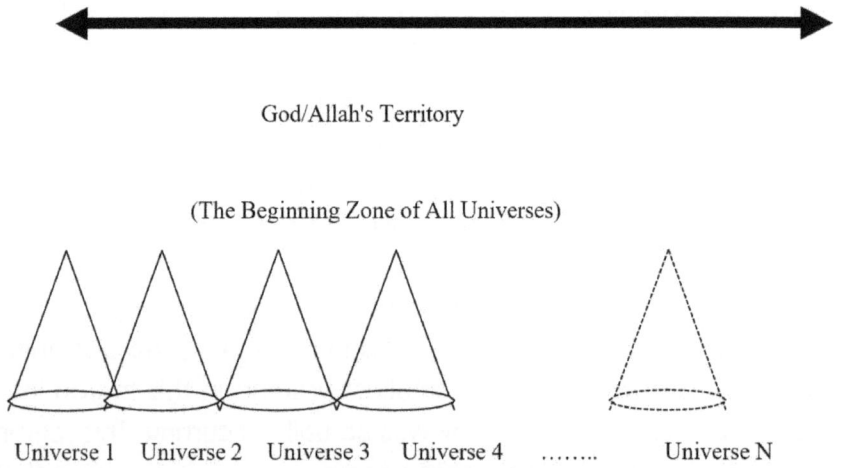

God/Allah's Territory

(The Beginning Zone of All Universes)

Universe 1   Universe 2   Universe 3   Universe 4   ....   Universe N

Figure 1

In the first phase, only 2 (two) ships with a total of 750 people on board were to set off for this purpose. Preparations were made and the equipment to be used was placed on the spaceships. Positive and a large number of robots were to be present on this trip. Only the positive and the robots would not be in the other two (2) ships, but in a different third ship. Everything was now ready for take-off and all three ships took off from their positions at the same time. The exploration, or in other words, the discovery, started immediately after the departure of their home planet. Every situation encountered or found was recorded, as different situations in different regions were then compared to find commonalities. This required memories with very large capacities. So much so that the recording speed in terms of capacity/time was X.XXX.XXX.XXX. XXX.XXX... PB/pico second. This means that whatever they came across would be recorded. The records (data) would then be processed to obtain information. The information would then be compared to see if different regions had common information or not. The answer to this question would be found. If there are, what are the common ones, these would be taken into different processes and at least one common feature of each existing volume (whether it contains anything or not) would be tried to be found. Thus, through this common feature, all kinds of communication would be established at the same time/ instantaneously, without any time delay. Spaceships traveled at very, very slow speeds compared to their normal speeds. Because everything would be recorded. If the speeds of the spaceships exceeded the data recording speeds in a functional sense, then some data would not be recorded. Therefore, the speed of the ships was around 1/2 of the recording speed. There was also a connection/relationship/function between the amount of data to be recorded and the volume of that data. In other words, the largest amount of data was to be recorded from the smallest volume previously agreed and selected. Naturally, there was data to be recorded. But it was necessary to know what this data was. In this case, many uncertainties come to the surface. Because everything that existed was not limited to the number of things they knew. It was an indisputable fact that there were an infinite number of facts, values, objects, events, etc. that they did not know. For this reason, a very, very large percentage of the data they received with their measurement or perception equipment was recorded as "explaining something unknown/ data of something unknown". Later, when the journey was over, the common information to be obtained by processing the data would be the value/explanation of "that unknown". Before going on the trip, everyone was sure that the common feature would be found and they also determined the word(s) they would name it when they found it. That phrase consisted of 7 (seven) words and was as follows: "partnership component from existence to extinction" (VOYOKOB). They expected to discover at least 1 (one) of these. It could have been more than 1 (one), this was not known at the time. All of those who went on the journey thought that their average life expectancy was 95 (ninety-five) years. Their average age at that moment was between 30 and 50. Since they would all return at the same time, they allocated a period of 25 to 30 years for the journey to find VOYOKOB. If 30 (thirty) years, the youngest would be 60 (sixty) and the oldest 80 (eighty) years old. They would spend the remaining period of 15 to 35 years working to realize instant communication through this VOYOKOB they had found. This was the plan they made and the plan they were going to implement. While the research ships were traveling, they would sometimes reach very high speeds and go to very remote areas and record data from there. They had set an average period for this. Every 2 (two) months, they would go to a region 1 (one) month away from their current location at the highest speed of the spaceship. This would become evident with the value obtained by taking the highest speed of the spaceship and 1 (one) month into a function and processing it. This has also been calculated before. When it was adapted to today's Solar System, the result was as follows: Approximately 70 (seventy) times the distance from the center of the Sun to the end of the Solar System (i.e. the boundary). Thus, the journey had started about 1.5 (one and a half) weeks ago and data recording was going on without interruption. In fact, since the number of data recording equipment on the spaceships would certainly not be sufficient to record all the data, the data would be transmitted to their planets through various/different communication methods and stored in the memory units there. Travelers would spend a significant part of their lives inside their spaceships. This does not mean that they would stay entirely inside the spaceship. Depending on the situation, they would also try to find the answers to a number of questions - if they came across planets suitable for life, what is different about them from their own planet, and so on. At that moment, they were as sure as they were that some of the data stored in the electronic equipment on their spacecraft and some of the data stored on their own planets by transmission were the VOYOKOB data they were trying to find. But which of the data they were trying to find, they could not answer at the time. (Also, the data was obtained with the location coordinates of the data. Thus, when they found the VOYOKOB, they would have found the path/line it followed/ encompassed/contained in the universe they were in. They would then be able to communicate easily over that line - after activating the hardware. -) In the next stage, when they created the mathematical function expressing this line/path, they would be able to predict the path/line of VOYOKOB in other universes, perhaps without going to other universes, by using the connection between it and their own universe. They would also be able to obtain from the data the width, length, height, etc. of that line/path. Finally, it was time to maximize the speed, because 2 (two) months were now behind us. Thus, all 3 (three) spaceships started their uninterrupted 1 (one) month journey at the highest speed, parallel to each other, in the same direction and in the same direction. The same engines were used in all 3 (three) ships. However, the number of engines differed according to the volume of the ship in question. In other words, one ship could travel at the highest speed with 2 (two) engines, while another ship could travel at the highest speed with 5 (five) engines. (Due to the volume differences of spaceships.) The one-month harpoon-speed journey was finally completed. In the meantime, data recording continued during this one (1) month. However, since the speed of the spaceships during this one month was much higher than the data recording speed of the equipment on board the ships, the data of every coordinates region passed along the way could not be obtained. In another sense, this was a structure that can be considered/evaluated as "sampling" a large number of data. This came and went in 1 (one) month and a total of 3 (three) months have passed. Since no one had left any of the spaceships at that moment, they were a little bit bored because they had been in a confined space for a long time. Therefore, as the journey continued, they were thinking, "I wish we could find a planet suitable for life so that we could land and walk a little bit inside the planet". It was not long before they reached this wish. After about 1 (one) week, the sensors of all 3 (three) spaceships detected that there was a planet suitable for life within a distance of 4 (four) days. (According to the speed of the spaceships at that moment.) The time in question came and went and the ships landed on the suitable planet in such a way that they were positioned side by side. All the living beings inside and some of the robots got out. Some robots remained inside the ship. "Just in case, just in case, if there were creatures on this alien planet and they wanted to attack and harm the ships... They stayed in the ships for protection." Again, the positive was at the front, followed by a large number of robots, and behind them the other creatures began to walk one after the other. The first thing they noticed were the tall trees on the planet, with no top or end visible from below. And they hadn't even walked 150 (one hundred and fifty) meters, they didn't count, but they saw 5-6 rivers flowing parallel to each other. Moreover, each river was flowing a different color liquid. As they continued walking, they were thinking, "Is this fruit juice or some kind of colored water or acid or a completely different type of liquid?" because of the different colors of the liquids flowing in the rivers. They did not carry any equipment with them to identify the liquids they encountered as they walked, so they did no more than stare at them as they flowed by. They had brought with them an ace number of robots assigned to protect them. Therefore, they positively thought to themselves, "I wonder what we will do if we face a large-scale attack, we don't know what's on the planet, so let's not stay here for long, let's walk a little more and then return to our ships and continue the VOYOKOB journey from where we left off." Positive was the first priority responsible for the whole team. After him came the others. They walked collectively for another half an hour or so, then retraced their steps and returned to the spaceships they had left. There were some who stayed on board and did not come out. After a short time, the three (3) ships took off and left the planet and the VOYOKOB journey started again from where it had left off. The speed of the ships was reduced again and they continued their journey at a speed similar to the walking speed of a turtle. Once again, the standard and obvious things started to be done. In the meantime, as in the logic of an airplane entering turbulence, each of the three (3) spacecraft occasionally entered volumes with different structures that they had never known and experienced before. Until they emerged from these volumes, the three (3) spacecraft were literally shaking like a boiling soup at high temperature. So much so that these shakes could sometimes be very, very violent. Because of this, everything inside the ship was tossed randomly and hit the inner surface of the ship like an arrow from a bow. Not only on the basis of the inanimate objects on board, but also the living things on board the ships were adversely affected by this situation. In fact, there were many officials who were seriously injured because they did not think about such a negative situation before they started their journey and then experienced it. They were immediately sent back to their planets with the incoming spaceships (for treatment.) There were sheltered sections in the ships. Until that moment they had not used them because they did not need them. But after that, if they encountered this or any other situation, they would use it in a 100 percent sense. But there were no precautions taken for inanimate objects in spacecraft. No matter how much they were stabilized, they could not avoid being thrown violently. In this case, a lot of important equipment was damaged by the impact, and even a large part of it was out of use. The equipment found in this situation was sent back to their planets by incoming spaceships and replaced with new ones. While the paths/regions they had taken were left behind, suddenly 3 (three) ships were almost stuck where they were, unable to move in any way. They first tried to understand what was causing this by examining the characteristics of the region they were stuck in with the equipment on board the ships. This is what they found out: "they were inside a cage. You can enter this cage/zone from the outside, but once you enter, you can't get out". The cage/zone in question was built with these features. They stayed in this way for about 2 (two) hours, when communication was established with the transmitters and receivers on board the ships. Positive also took over the communication of other ships. An alien being appeared on the receiver screen and said: "You have entered a disputed territory between us and an enemy planet. If any ship other than our own ships enters this zone, it cannot leave again without our permission. We know that you are not ships belonging to our enemy planet. Where did you come from, where are you going and why did you enter the area we call our - red line - and what is your purpose?" Affirmative: "We come to you from a star system many months away. We have no specific destination. We have embarked on such a journey for scientific purposes. We have entered this - red line - zone of yours by chance. We have no malicious intentions. Let us get out of here and we will leave and continue on our way with our purpose". Live on the receiver: "first we will check your ships, then we will decide." Positive: "what do you expect to find on our ships, we have weapons for self-defense and tools and equipment for our research". The creature in the receiver: "If you leave all the weapons on all 3 (three) ships in the area you are in now, then we will make sure you get out of here." Affirmative: "but in that case, if we face any attack on our journey, then we will be defenseless because we have no weapons. I cannot accept that." Live on receiver: "then we will take your weapons by force. Either hand them over voluntarily or we will come and take them by force." Affirmative: "ok fine, after 15 (fifteen) minutes, all the weapons on all 3 (three) ships will be taken out of the ships". Affirmative: "Alright, a spaceship of ours is about to reach your location. Your weapons will be taken to this ship and then your ships will be taken out of this area". And after about 25 (twenty-five) minutes, the weapons in question were taken on board the incoming ship and then 3 (three) ships were allowed to leave the area. Then the VOYOKOB voyage, which had a pause period, started again. When they communicated with the electronic equipment on board the ships while the voyage continued, the common theme was: there are no weapons left on any ship, we are completely defenseless. If there is any attack against us, we cannot respond to it. After that, there was nothing left for us to do but pray to God/Allah that we would not encounter any enemies for the rest of our journey. It had been 8 (eight) months since the journey began. After this period, 3 (three) ships were being pursued by dozens of unknown spaceships coming from behind. They tried to communicate with these ships, but they did not receive any response to the signals they sent. After a while, he made a positive decision: "since we are vulnerable, I think we should not continue and go back to our planet". The others agreed with the affirmative's thinking. But there was one thing they were thinking, and it was true. "They wanted to go back, but would they succeed?" They themselves did not know the answer to that. Because the group of spaceships coming from behind formed a spherical structure among themselves and took the 3 (three) ships into it. At this very moment, the three (3) ships were hit by a very powerful and intense laser beam. Even though the outer surface of the ships was solid and reflective, it could not withstand the incoming beams any longer and began to melt like ice under the influence of sunlight. All 3 (three) ships did not have an escape plan in place when their ships became unusable. Therefore, all those on board perished after the laser beam reached their bodies. Thus, an unknown region of the universe they were in became their "place of death". The journey they set out on to conduct scientific research ended with their deaths. Before they died, they could not establish any communication with their home planet. So those who stayed on the planet were left wondering "where did those who left stay, why didn't they return, when will they return, did something bad happen to them? They were left with unanswered questions.

May 01, 2024 - Wednesday, 15:00
Lect. Assoc. (Computer Eng.) METİN ŞAHİN